He loved to hear the bees humming and the
birds singing. *Page 13*.

CHILDREN'S THRIFT CLASSICS

Tommy and the Wishing-Stone

THORNTON W. BURGESS

Illustrated by Harrison Cady

PUBLISHED IN ASSOCIATION WITH THE
THORNTON W. BURGESS SOCIETY,
SANDWICH, MASSACHUSETTS
BY
DOVER PUBLICATIONS, INC.
MINEOLA, NEW YORK

DOVER CHILDREN'S THRIFT CLASSICS

EDITOR OF THIS VOLUME: JANET BAINE KOPITO

Copyright

This Dover edition, first published by Dover Publications, Inc., in 2011 in association with the Thornton Burgess Society, Sandwich, Massachusetts, who have provided a new Introduction, is an unabridged republication of the work originally published by The Century Company, New York, in 1915.

Library of Congress Cataloging-in-Publication Data

Burgess, Thornton W.
   Tommy and the wishing stone / Thornton W. Burgess ; illustrated by Harrison Cady.
       p. cm. — (Dover's children's thrift classics)
   Summary: Tommy is sulking when he happens to sit upon a stone that unexpectedly grants his wish, allowing him to experience life as a series of woodland creatures, including a mouse, a bird, a mink, and a toad.
   ISBN-13: 978-0-486-48105-0
   ISBN-10: 0-486-48105-0
   [1. Forest animals — Fiction.   2. Nature — Fiction.] 1. Cady, Harrison, 1877–1970, ill.

PZ7.B917 Tom 2011
[E]—dc22

                                                                2011036100

Manufactured in the United States by LSC Communications
48105004   2018
www.doverpublications.com

TO the cause of love, mercy and protection
for our little friends of the air and the wild-wood
and to a better understanding of them
this little book is dedicated.

THE AUTHOR

Introduction to the Dover Edition

The twelve stories in *Tommy and the Wishing-Stone* were originally serialized in *St. Nicholas* magazine from November 1914 to October 1915. *St. Nicholas* magazine, published from 1873 until 1941, was dedicated to inspiring young people between the ages of five and eighteen to appreciate the world around them and to think realistically about it. Created by Scribner's, it passed to The Century Company of New York in 1881. They published it until 1933, when economics forced them to merge with D. Appleton Company. The Century Company's field of expertise was actually history, but they were known for the high quality of their efforts in all of their endeavors. Some other stories serialized in *St. Nicholas* were "Little Jo" by Louisa May Alcott and "The Jungle Stories" by Rudyard Kipling.

After the "Wishing-Stone" stories' successful run in *St. Nicholas* magazine, The Century Company immediately republished all twelve stories as a single book, *Tommy and the Wishing-Stone*. In 1921, Little, Brown, and Company bought the rights and divided the stories up into three volumes, called "The Wishing Stone Series." In 1935, Little, Brown and Company recombined all the stories in one book, *The Wishing-Stone Stories.* The publishing house of Grosset and Dunlap got their chance in 1959, and once again divided the stories into three books.

In Thornton Burgess's "Tommy and the Wishing Stone" stories, Tommy—Farmer Brown's boy—does a lot of growing up. He starts out as the lazy, thoughtless boy we met in Burgess's first book, *Old Mother West Wind.* At the beginning of the first story in *Tommy and the Wishing-Stone*, he is immersed in self-pity. Burgess's observations about the causes of his condition will make adults smile as much now as they first did ninety-five years ago. Some things about human nature never change.

As the stories progress, Tommy learns about the joys and perils experienced by the various inhabitants of the Green Meadows and the Green Forest. Initially thinking the creatures to be carefree and fair game for his own amusement, he comes to realize how hard it is to be a wild animal and regrets the ways he has added to their tribulations. Burgess was never a friend to hunters, and *Tommy and the Wishing-Stone* is his most consistent indictment of the practice. His view is now so widely accepted, it is hard to remember how new it was when he wrote the stories: At that time, there was no such thing as a hunting "season" in the United

States. There would not be one for another four years, and Burgess would be instrumental in bringing it about.

JOHN RICHMOND
The Thornton W. Burgess Society
Sandwich, Massachusetts

Contents

List of Illustrations

Tommy and the Wishing-Stone

I
Tommy and the Wishing-Stone

TOMMY scuffed his bare, brown feet in the grass and didn't even notice how cooling and refreshing to his bare toes the green blades were. Usually he just loved to feel them, but this afternoon he just didn't want to find anything pleasant or nice in the things he was accustomed to. A scowl, a deep, dark, heavy scowl, had chased all merriment from his round, freckled face. It seemed as if the very freckles were trying to hide from it. Tommy didn't care. He said so. He said so right out loud. He didn't care if all the world knew it. He wanted the world to know it. It was a horrid old world anyway, this world which made a fellow go hunt up and drive home a lot of pesky cows just when all the other fellows were over at the swimming-hole. It always was that way whenever there was anything interesting or particular to do, or any fun going on. Yes, it was a horrid old world, this world in which Tommy lived, and he was quite willing that everybody should know it.

The truth was, Tommy was deep, very deep, in the sulks. He was so deep in them that he couldn't see jolly round Mr. Sun smiling down on him. He couldn't see anything lovely in the beautiful, broad, Green Meadows with the shadows of the clouds chasing

1

one another across them. He couldn't hear the music of the birds and the bees. He couldn't even hear the Merry Little Breezes whispering secrets as they danced around him. He couldn't see and hear because—well, because he *wouldn't* see and hear. That is always the way with people who go way down deep in the sulks.

Presently he came to a great big stone. Tommy stopped and scowled at it just as he had been scowling at everybody and everything. He scowled at it as if he thought it had no business to be there. Yet all the time he was glad that it was there. It was just the right size to sit on and make himself happy by being perfectly miserable. You know, some people actually find pleasure in thinking how miserable they are. The more miserable they can make themselves feel, the sooner they begin to pity themselves, and when they begin to pity themselves they seem to find what Uncle Jason calls a "melancholy pleasure." It was that way with Tommy. Because no one else seemed to pity him, he wanted to pity himself, and to do that right he must first make himself feel the most miserable he possibly could. So he sat down on the big stone, waved his stick for a few moments and then threw it away, put his chin in his two hands and his two elbows on his two knees, and began by scowling down at his bare, brown toes.

"There's never anything to do around here, and when there is, a fellow can't do it," he grumbled.

Tommy is happy by being perfectly miserable. *Page 2.*

"Other fellows don't have to weed the garden, and bring in wood, and drive the cows, and when they do it, it ain't just when they want to have some fun. What's vacation for, if it ain't to have a good time in? And how's a fellow going to do it when he has to work all the time—anyway when he has to work just when he don't want to?" He was trying to be truthful.

"Fellows who live in town have something going on all the time, while out here there's nothing but fields, and woods, and sky, and—and cows that haven't sense enough to come home themselves when it's time. There's never anything exciting or int'resting 'round here. I wish—"

He suddenly became aware of two very small bright eyes watching him from a little opening in the grass. He scowled at them harder than ever, and moved ever so little. The eyes disappeared, but a minute later they were back again, full of curiosity, a little doubtful, a little fearful, but tremendously interested. They were the eyes of Danny Meadow Mouse. Tommy knew them right away. Of course he did. Hadn't he chased Danny with sticks and stones time and again? But he didn't think of this now. He was too full of his own troubles to remember that others had troubles too.

Somehow Danny's twinkling little eyes seemed to mock him. How unjust things were!

"*You* don't have to work!" he exploded so suddenly and fiercely that Danny gave a frightened squeak and took to his heels. "You don't have anything to do but play all day and have a good time. I wish I was a meadow-mouse!"

Right then and there something happened, Tommy didn't know how it happened, but it just did. Instead of a bare-legged, freckle-faced, sulky boy sitting on the big stone, he suddenly found himself a little, chunky, blunt-headed, furry animal with four ridiculously short stubby legs, and he was scampering after Danny Meadow Mouse along a private little path through the meadow-grass. He was a meadow-mouse himself! His wish had come true!

Tommy felt very happy. He had forgotten that he ever was a boy. He raced along the private little path just as if he had always been accustomed to just such private little paths. It might be very hot out in the sun, but down there among the sheltering grass stems it was delightfully cool and comfortable. He tried to shout for very joy, but what he really did do was to squeak. It was a thin, sharp little squeak. It was answered right away from in front of him, and Tommy didn't like the sound of it. Being a meadow-mouse now, he understood the speech of meadow-mice, and he knew that Danny Meadow Mouse was demanding to know who was running in his private little path. Tommy suspected by the angry sound of Danny's voice that he meant to fight.

Tommy hesitated. Then he stopped. He didn't want to fight. You see, he knew that he had no business on that path without an invitation from the owner. If it had been his own path he would have been eager to fight. But it wasn't, and so he thought it best to avoid trouble. He turned and scampered back a little way to a tiny branch path. He followed this until it also branched, and then took the new path. But none of these paths really belonged to him. He wanted some of his very own. Now the only way to have a private path of your very own in the Green Meadows is to make it, unless you are big enough and strong enough to take one away from some one else.

So Tommy set to work to make a path of his own, and he did it by cutting the grass one stem at a time. The very tender ones he ate. The rest he carried to an old board he had discovered, and under this he made a nest, using the finest, softest grasses for the inside. Of course it was work. As a matter of fact, had he, as a boy, had to work one-tenth as much or as hard as he now had to work as a meadow-mouse, he would have felt sure that he was the most abused boy who ever lived. But, being a meadow-mouse, he didn't think anything about it, and scurried back and forth as fast as ever he could, just stopping now and then to rest. He knew that he must work for everything he had—that without work he would have nothing. And somehow this all seemed perfectly right. He was busy, and in keeping busy he kept happy.

Presently, as he sat down to rest a minute, a Merry Little Breeze came hurrying along, and brought with it just the faintest kind of a sound. It made his heart jump. Every little unexpected sound made his heart jump. He listened with all his might. There it was again! Something was stealing very, very softly through the grass. He felt sure it was danger of some kind. Then he did a foolish thing—he ran. You see, he was so frightened that he felt that he just couldn't sit still a second longer, so he ran. The instant he moved, something big and terrible sprang at him, and two great paws with sharp claws spread out all but landed on him. He gave a frightened squeak, and darted under an old fence-post that lay half hidden in the tall grass.

"What's the matter with you?" demanded a voice. Tommy found that he had company. It was another meadow-mouse.

"I—I've had such a narrow escape!" panted Tommy. "A terrible creature with awful claws almost caught me!"

The stranger peeped out to see. "Pooh!" said he, "that was only a cat. Cats don't know much. If you keep your ears and eyes open, it's easy enough to fool cats. But they are a terrible nuisance just the same, because they are always prowling around when you least expect them. I hate cats! It is bad enough to have to watch out all the time for enemies who live on the Green Meadows, without having to be always looking to see if a cat is about. A cat hasn't any excuse at all. It has all it wants to eat without trying to catch us. It hunts just out of love of cruelty.

Now Reddy Fox has some excuse; he has to eat. Too bad he's so fond of meadow-mice. Speaking of Reddy, have you seen him lately?"

Tommy shook his head. "I guess it's safe enough to go out now," continued the stranger. "I know where there is a dandy lot of corn; let's go get some."

Tommy was quite willing. The stranger led the way. First he looked this way and that way, and listened for any sound of danger. Tommy did likewise. But the way seemed clear, and away they scampered. Right away Tommy was happy again. He had forgotten his recent fright. That is the way with little people of the Green Meadows. But he didn't forget to keep his ears and his eyes wide open for new dangers. They reached the corn safely, and then such a feast as they did have! It seemed to Tommy that never had he tasted anything half so good. Right in the midst of the feast, the stranger gave a faint little squeak and darted under a pile of old cornstalks. Tommy didn't stop to ask questions, but followed right at his heels. A big, black shadow swept over them and then passed on. Tommy peeped out. There was a great bird with huge, broad wings sailing back and forth over the meadows.

"It's old Whitetail, the Marsh Hawk. He didn't get us that time!" chuckled the stranger, and crept back to the delicious corn. In two minutes, they were having as good a time as before, just as if they hadn't had a narrow escape. When they had eaten all they could hold, the stranger went back to his old fence-post and Tommy returned to his own private paths and the snug nest he had built under the old board. He was sleepy, and he curled up for a good long nap.

When he awoke, the first stars were beginning to twinkle down at him from the sky, and black shadows lay over the Green Meadows. He found that he could see quite as well as in the light of day, and, because he was already hungry again, he started out to look for something to eat. Something inside warned him that he must watch out for danger now just as sharply as before, though the black shadows seemed to promise safety. Just what he was to watch out for he didn't know, but still every few steps he stopped to look and listen. He found that this was visiting time among the meadow-mice, and he made a great many friends. There was a great deal of scurrying back and forth along private little paths, and a great deal of squeaking. At least, that is what Tommy would have called it if he had still been a boy, but as it was, he understood it perfectly, for it was meadow-mouse language. Suddenly there was not a sound to be heard, not a single squeak or the sound of scurrying feet. Tommy sat perfectly still and held his breath. He didn't know why, but something inside told him to, and he did. Then something passed over him. It was like a great shadow, and it was just as silent as a shadow. But Tommy knew that it wasn't a shadow, for out of it two great, round, fierce, yellow eyes glared down and struck such terror to his heart that it almost stopped beating. But

It was visiting time and he made a great many friends. *Page 9.*

they didn't see him, and he gave a tiny sigh of relief as he watched the grim living shadow sail on. While he watched, there was a frightened little squeak, two legs with great curved claws dropped down from the shadow, plunged into the grass, and when they came up again they held a little limp form. A little mouse had moved when he shouldn't have, and Hooty the Owl had caught a dinner.

A dozen times that night Tommy sat quite frozen with fear while Hooty passed, but after each time he joined with his fellows in merrymaking just as if there was no such thing as this terrible feathered hunter with the silent wings, only each one was ready to hide at the first sign of danger. When he grew tired of playing and eating, he returned to his snug nest under the old board to sleep. He was still asleep there the next morning when, without any warning, the old board was lifted. In great fright Tommy ran out of his nest, and at once there was a great shout from a huge giant, who struck at him with a stick and then chased him, throwing sticks and stones, none of which hit him, but which frightened him terribly. He dodged down a little path and ran for his life, while behind him he heard the giant (it was just a boy) shouting and laughing as he poked about in the grass trying to find poor Tommy, and Tommy wondered what he could be laughing about, and what fun there could be in frightening a poor little meadow-mouse almost to death.

Hooty the Owl. *Page 11*.

Later that very same morning, while he was hard at work cutting a new path, he heard footsteps behind him, and turned to see a big, black bird stalking along the little path. He didn't wait for closer acquaintance, but dived into the thick grass, and, as he did so, the big, black bird made a lunge at him, but missed him. It was his first meeting with Blacky the Crow, and he had learned of one more enemy to watch out for.

But most of all he feared Reddy Fox. He never could be quite sure when Reddy was about. Sometimes it would be in broad daylight, and sometimes in the stilly night. The worst of it was, Reddy seemed to know all about the ways of meadow-mice, and would lie perfectly still beside a little path until an unsuspecting mouse came along. Then there would be a sudden spring, a little squeak cut short right in the middle, and there would be one less happy little worker and playmate. So Tommy learned to look and listen before he started for any place, and then to scurry as fast as ever he could.

Twice Mr. Gopher-snake almost caught him, and once he got away from Billy Mink by squeezing into a hole between some roots too small for Billy to get in. It was a very exciting life, very exciting indeed. He couldn't understand why, when all he wanted was to be allowed to mind his own business and work and play in peace, he must be forever running or hiding for his life. He loved the sweet meadow-grasses and the warm sunshine. He loved to hear

Blacky the Crow. *Page 13.*

the bees humming and the birds singing. He thought the Green Meadows the most beautiful place in all the great world, and he was very happy when he wasn't frightened; but there was hardly an hour of the day or night that he didn't have at least one terrible fright.

Still, it was good to be alive and explore new places. There was a big rock in front of him right now. He wondered if there was anything to eat on top of it. Sometimes he found the very nicest seeds in the cracks of big rocks. This one looked as if it would not be very hard to scramble up on. He felt almost sure that he would find some treasure up there. He looked this way and that way to make sure no one was watching. Then he scrambled up on the big rock.

For a few minutes, Tommy stared out over the Green Meadows. They were very beautiful. It seemed to him that they never had been so beautiful, or the songs of the birds so sweet, or the Merry Little Breezes, the children of Old Mother West Wind, so soft and caressing. He couldn't understand it all, for he wasn't a meadow-mouse—just a barefooted boy sitting on a big stone that was just made to sit on. As he looked down, he became aware of two very small bright eyes watching him from a little opening in the grass. He knew them right away. Of course he did. They were the eyes of Danny Meadow Mouse. They were filled with curiosity, a little doubtful, a little fearful, but tremendously interested.

Tommy smiled, and felt in his pocket for some cracker-crumbs. Danny ran away at the first move, but Tommy scattered the crumbs where he could find them, as he was sure to come back.

Tommy stood up and stretched. Then he turned and looked curiously at the stone on which he had been sitting. "I believe it's a real wishing-stone," said he. Then he laughed aloud. "I'm glad I'm not a meadow-mouse, but just a boy!" he cried. "I guess those cows are wondering what has become of me." He started toward the pasture, and now there was no frown darkening his freckled face. It was clear and good to see, and he whistled as he tramped along. Once he stopped and grinned sheepishly as his blue eyes drank in the beauty of the Green Meadows and beyond them the Green Forest. "And I said there was nothing interesting or exciting going on here! Why, it's the most exciting place I ever heard of, only I didn't know it before!" he muttered. "Gee, I *am* glad I'm not a meadow-mouse, and if ever I throw sticks or stones at one again, I—well, I hope I turn into one!"

And though Danny Meadow Mouse, timidly nibbling at the cracker-crumbs, didn't know it, he had one less enemy to be afraid of!

II
Why Tommy Became a Friend of Red Squirrels

"I DON'T see what Sis wants to string this stuff all over the house for, just because it happens to be Christmas!" grumbled Tommy, as he sat on a big stone and idly kicked at a pile of beautiful ground-pine and fragrant balsam boughs. "It's the best day for skating we've had yet, and here I am missing a whole morning of it, and so tired that most likely I won't feel like going this afternoon!"

Now Tommy knew perfectly well that if his mother said that he could go, nothing could keep him away from the pond that afternoon. He was a little tired, perhaps, but not nearly so tired as he tried to think he was. Gathering Christmas greens was work of course. But when you come right down to it, there is work about almost everything, even skating. The chief difference between work and pleasure is the difference between "must" and "want to." When you *must* do a thing it becomes work; when you *want* to do a thing it becomes pleasure.

Right down deep inside, where his honest self lives, Tommy was glad that there was going to be a green wreath in each of the front windows, and that over the doors and pictures there would be sweet-smelling balsam. Without them, why, Christmas wouldn't be Christmasy at all! And really it had been fun gathering those greens. He wouldn't admit it, but it had. He wouldn't have missed it for the world. It was only that it had to be done just when he wanted to do something else. And so he tried to feel grieved and persecuted, and to forget that Christmas was only two days off.

He sat on the big gray stone and looked across the Green Meadows, no longer green but covered with the whitest and lightest of snow-blankets, across the Old Pasture, not one whit less beautiful, to the Green Forest, and he sighed. It was a deep, heavy sigh. It was the sigh of a self-made martyr. As if in reply, he heard the sharp voice of Chatterer the Red-Squirrel. It rang out clear and loud on the frosty air, and it was very plain that, whatever troubles others might have, Chatterer was very well satisfied with the world in general and himself in particular. Just now he was racing along the fence, stopping at every post to sit up and tell all the world that he was there and didn't care who knew it. Presently his sharp eyes spied Tommy.

Chatterer stopped short in the middle of a rail and looked at Tommy very hard. Then he barked at him, jerking his tail with every syllable. Tommy didn't move. Chatterer jumped down from the fence and came nearer. Every foot or so he paused and barked, and his bark was such a funny mixture of nervousness and excitement and curiosity and sauciness, not to say impudence, that finally Tommy laughed right out. He just couldn't help it.

Back to the fence rushed Chatterer, and scampered up to the top of a post. Once sure of the safety of this retreat, he faced Tommy and began to scold as fast as his tongue could go. Of course Tommy couldn't understand what Chatterer was saying, but he could guess. He was telling Tommy just what he thought of a boy who would sit moping on such a beautiful day, and only two days before Christmas at that! My, how his tongue did fly! When he had had his say to the full, he gave a final whisk of his tail and scampered off in the direction of the Old Orchard. And, as he went, it seemed to Tommy as if he looked back with the sauciest kind of a twinkle in his eyes, as much as to say, "You deserve all I've said, but I don't really mean it!"

Tommy watched him, a lively little red spot against the white background, and, as he watched, the smile gradually faded away. It never would do at all to go home in good spirits after raising all the fuss he had created when he started out. So, to make himself feel as badly as he felt that he ought to feel, Tommy sighed dolefully.

"Oh, but you're lucky!" said he, as Chatterer's sharp voice floated over to him from the Old Orchard. "You don't have to do a blessed thing unless you want to! All you have to do is to eat and sleep and have a good time. It must be fun. I wish I were a squirrel!"

Right then something happened. It happened all in a flash, just as it had happened to Tommy once before. One minute he was a boy, a discontented boy, sitting on a big gray stone on the edge of the Green Meadows, and the next minute he wasn't a boy at all! You see, when he made that wish, he had quite forgotten that he was sitting on the wishing-stone. Now he no longer had to guess at what Chatterer was saying. Not a bit of it. He knew. He talked the same language himself. In short, he was a red squirrel, and in two minutes had forgotten that he ever had been a boy.

How good it felt to be free and know that he could do just as he pleased! His first impulse was to race over to the Old Orchard and make the acquaintance of Chatterer. Then he thought better of it. Something inside him seemed to tell him that he had no business there—that the Old Orchard was not big enough for two red squirrels, and that, as Chatterer had gone there first, it really belonged to him in a way. He felt quite sure of it when he had replied to Chatterer's sharp voice, and had been told in no uncertain tones that the best thing he could do would be to run right back where he had come from.

Of course, he couldn't do that, so he decided to do the next best thing—run over to the Green Forest and see what there was to do there. He hopped up on the rail fence and whisked along the top rail.

What fun it was! He didn't have a care in the world. All he had to do was to eat, drink, and have

a good time. Ha! who was that coming along behind him! Was it Chatterer? It looked something like
him, and yet different somehow. Tommy sat quite
still watching the stranger, and, as he watched,
a curious terror began to creep over him. The
stranger wasn't Chatterer. No, indeed, he wasn't
even a squirrel! He was too long and slim, and
his tail was different. He was Shadow the Weasel!
Tommy didn't have to be told that. Although he
never had seen Shadow before, he knew without being told. For a minute he couldn't move.
Then, his heart beating with fear until it seemed
as if it would burst, he fled along the fence toward
the Green Forest, and now he didn't stop at the
posts when he came to them. His one thought
was to get away, away as far as ever he could; for
in the eyes of Shadow the Weasel he had seen
death.

Up the nearest tree he raced and hid, clinging
close to the trunk near the top, staring down with
eyes fairly bulging with fright. Swiftly, yet without
seeming to hurry, Shadow the Weasel came straight
to the tree in which Tommy was hiding, his nose
in Tommy's tracks in the way that a hound follows
a rabbit or a fox. At the foot of the tree he stopped
just a second and looked up. Then he began to climb.
At the first scratch of his claws on the bark Tommy
raced out along a branch and leaped across to the
next tree. Then, in a great panic, he went on from
tree to tree, taking desperate chances in his long

Tommy sat quite still watching the stranger. *Page 21.*

leaps. In the whole of his little being he had room for but one feeling, and that was fear—fear of that savage pitiless pursuer.

He had run a long way before he realized that he was no longer being followed. The fact is, Shadow had found other game, easier to catch, and had given up. Now, just as soon as Tommy realized that Shadow the Weasel was no longer on his track, he straightway forgot his fear. In fact it was just as if he never had had a fright, for that is the law of Nature with her little people of the wild. So presently Tommy was once more as happy and care-free as before.

In a big chestnut-tree just ahead of him he could see Happy Jack the Gray Squirrel; and Happy Jack was very busy about something. Perhaps he had a storehouse there. The very thought made Tommy hungry. Once more he hid, but this time not in fear. He hid so that he could watch Happy Jack. Not a sound did he make as he peered out from his hiding-place. Happy Jack was a long time in that hollow limb! It seemed as if he never would come out. So Tommy started on to look for more mischief, for he was bubbling over with good spirits and felt that he must do something.

Presently, quite by accident, he discovered another hoard of nuts, mostly acorns, neatly tucked away in a crotch of a big tree. Of course he sampled them. "What fun!" thought he. "I don't know whose they are, and I don't care. From now on, they are going to belong to me." He started to carry them away, but a sudden harsh scream close to him started him so that he dropped the nut he had in his mouth. He dodged behind the trunk of the tree just in time to escape the dash of an angry bird in a brilliant blue suit with white and black trimmings.

"Thief! thief! thief! Leave my nuts alone!" screamed Sammy Jay, anger making his voice harsher than ever.

Round and round the trunk of the tree Tommy dodged, chattering back in reply to the sharp tongue of the angry jay. It was exciting without being very dangerous. After a while, however, it grew tiresome, and, watching his chance, he slipped over to another tree and into a hole made by Drummer the Woodpecker. Sammy Jay didn't see where he had disappeared, and, after hunting in vain, gave up and began to carry his nuts away to a new hiding-place. Tommy's eyes sparkled with mischief as he watched. By and by he would have a hunt for it! It would be fun!

When Sammy Jay had hidden the last nut and flown away, Tommy came out. He didn't feel like hunting for those nuts just then, so he scampered up in a tall hemlock-tree, and, just out of sheer good spirits and because he could see no danger near, he called sharply that all within hearing might know that he was about. Almost instantly he received a reply from not far away. It was an angry warning to keep away from that part of the Green Forest,

A sudden harsh scream startled him so
that he dropped the nut. *Page 24*.

because he had no business there! It was the voice of Chatterer. Tommy replied just as angrily that he would stay if he wanted to. Then they barked and chattered at each other for a long time. Gradually Chatterer came nearer. Finally he was in the very next tree. He stopped there long enough to tell Tommy all that he would do to him when he caught him, and at the end he jumped across to Tommy's tree.

Tommy waited no longer. He wasn't ready to fight. In the first place he knew that Chatterer probably had lived there a long time, and so was partly right in saying that Tommy had no business there. Then Chatterer looked a little the bigger and stronger. So Tommy nimbly ran out on a branch and leaped across to the next tree. In a flash Chatterer was after him, and then began a most exciting race through the tree-tops. Tommy found that there were regular squirrel highways through the tree-tops, and along these he raced at top speed, Chatterer at his heels, scolding and threatening. When he reached the edge of the Green Forest, Tommy darted down the last tree, across the open space to the old stone wall, and along this Chatterer followed.

Suddenly the anger in Chatterer's voice changed to a sharp cry of warning. Tommy scrambled into a crevice between two stones without stopping to inquire what the trouble was. When he peeped out, he saw a great bird sailing back and forth. In a few minutes it lighted on a near-by tree, and sat there

He saw a great bird sailing back and forth. *Page 26*.

so still that, if Tommy had not seen it light, he never would have known it was there.

"Mr. Goshawk nearly got you that time," said a voice very near at hand. Tommy turned to find Chatterer peeping out from another crevice in the old wall. "It won't be safe for us to show ourselves until he leaves," continued Chatterer. "It's getting so that an honest squirrel needs eyes in the back of his head to keep his skin whole, not to mention living out his natural life. Hello! here comes a boy, and that means more trouble. There's one good thing about it, and that is he'll frighten away that hawk."

Tommy looked, and sure enough there was a boy, and in his hands was an air-rifle. Tommy didn't know what it was, but Chatterer did.

"I wish that hawk would hurry up and fly so that we can run!" he sputtered. "The thing that boy carries throws things, and they hurt. It isn't best to let him get too near when he has that with him. He seems to think it's fun to hurt us. I'd just like to bite him once and see if he thought *that* was fun! There goes that hawk. Come on now, we've got to run for it!"

Chatterer led the way and Tommy followed. He was frightened, but there wasn't that terror which had possessed him when Shadow the Weasel was after him. Something struck sharply against the wall just behind him. It frightened him into greater speed. Something struck just in front of him, and then something hit him so hard that just for a second he nearly lost his balance. It hurt dreadfully.

"Hurrah!" shouted the boy, "I hit him that time!" Then the boy started to run after them so as to get a closer shot.

"We'll get up in the top of that big hemlock-tree and he won't be able to see us," panted Chatterer. "Did he hit you? That's too bad. It might have been worse though. If he had had one of those things that make a big noise and smoke, we might not either of us be here now. Boys are hateful things. I don't see what fun they get out of frightening and hurting such little folks as you and me. They're brutes! That's what they are! When we get across that little open place, we can laugh at him. Come on now!"

Down from the end of the old wall Chatterer jumped and raced across to the foot of a big hemlock-tree, Tommy at his heels. Up the tree they ran and hid close to the trunk where the branches were thick. They could peer down and see the boy, but he couldn't see them. He walked around the tree two or three times, and then shot up into the top to try to frighten the squirrels.

"Don't move!" whispered Chatterer. "He doesn't see us."

Tommy obeyed, although he felt as if he must run. His heart seemed to jump every time a bullet spatted in among the branches. It was dreadful to sit there and do nothing while being shot at, and not know but that the very next minute one of those little lead shots would hit. Tommy knew just how it would hurt if it did hit. Presently the boy gave up and went off to torment some one else. No sooner was his back fairly turned than Chatterer began to scold and jeer at him. Tommy joined him. It was just as if there never had been any danger. If that boy could have understood what they said, his ears would have burned.

Then Chatterer showed Tommy just what part of the Green Forest he claimed as his own, and also showed him a part that had belonged to another squirrel to whom something had happened, and suggested that Tommy take that for his. It wasn't as good as Chatterer's, but still it would do very well. Tommy took possession at once. Each agreed not to intrude on the other's territory. On common ground, that didn't belong to either of them, they would be the best of friends, but Tommy knew that if he went into Chatterer's part of the Green Forest, he would have to fight, and he made up his mind that if any other squirrel came into *his* part of the Green Forest, there would be a fight. Suddenly he was very jealous of his new possession. He was hardly willing to leave it when Chatterer suggested a visit to a near-by corn-crib for a feast of yellow corn.

Chatterer led the way. Tommy found that he was quite lame from the shot which had hit him, but he was soon racing after Chatterer again.

Along the old stone wall, then along a fence, up a maple-tree, and from there to the roof of the corn-crib, they scampered. Chatterer knew just where to get inside, and in a few minutes they were stuffing themselves with yellow corn. When they had eaten all that they could hold, they stuffed their cheeks full and started back the way they had come. Tommy went straight to his own part of the Green Forest, and there he hid his treasure, some in a hollow stump, and some under a little pile of leaves between the roots of a tree. All the time he watched sharply to make sure that no one saw him. While looking for new hiding-places, his nose told him to dig. There, buried under the leaves, he found nuts hidden by the one who had lived there before him. There must be a lot more hidden there, and it would be great fun hunting for them. Doubtless he would find as many as if he had hidden them himself, for he had seen that Chatterer didn't know where he had put a tenth part of the things *he* had hidden. He just trusted to his nose to help him get them again.

He found a splendid nest made of leaves and strips of inner bark in the hollow stub of a big branch of a chestnut-tree, and he made up his mind that there was where he would sleep. Then he ran over to see Chatterer again. He found him scolding at a cat who watched him with yellow, unblinking eyes. He would run down the trunk of the tree almost to the ground, and there scold and call names as fast as his tongue could go. Then he would run back up

Each agreed not to intrude on the other's territory. *Page 30.*

to the lowest branch and scold from there. The next time he would go a little farther down. Finally he leaped to the ground, and raced across to another tree. The cat sprang, but was just too late. Chatterer jeered at her. Then he began the same thing over again, and kept at it until finally the cat gave up and left in disgust. It had been exciting, but Tommy shivered at the thought of what might have happened.

"Ever try that with a fox?" asked Chatterer.

"No," replied Tommy.

"I have!" boasted Chatterer. "But I've seen squirrels caught doing it," he added. "Still, I suppose one may as well be caught by a fox as by a hawk."

"Did you see that weasel this morning?" asked Tommy.

Chatterer actually shivered as he replied: "Yes, I saw him after you. It's a wonder he didn't get you. You're lucky! I was lucky myself this morning, for a mink went right past where I was hiding. Life is nothing but one jump after another these days. It seems as if, when one has worked as hard as I did last fall to store up enough food to keep me all winter, I ought to be allowed to enjoy it in comfort. Those who sleep all winter, like Johnny Chuck, have a mighty easy time of it. They don't know when they are well off. Still, I'd hate to miss all the excitement and fun of life. I would rather jump for my life twenty times a day as I have to, and know that I'm alive, than to be alive and not know it. See that dog down there? I hate dogs! I'm going to tell him so."

Off raced Chatterer to bark and scold at a little black-and-white dog which paid no attention to him at all. The shadows were creeping through the trees, and Tommy began to think of his nest. He looked once more at Chatterer, who was racing along the top of the old wall scolding at the dog. Suddenly what seemed like merely a darker shadow swept over Chatterer, and, when it had passed, he had vanished. For once, that fatal once, he had been careless. Hooty the Owl had caught him. Tommy shivered. He was frightened and cold. He would get to his nest as quickly as he could. He leaped down to a great gray stone, and—behold, he wasn't a squirrel at all! He was just a boy sitting on a big stone, with a heap of Christmas greens at his feet.

He shivered, for he was cold. Then he jumped up and stamped his feet and threshed his arms. A million diamond points glittered in the white meadows where the snow crystals splintered the sunbeams. From the Old Orchard sounded the sharp scolding chirr and cough of Chatterer the Red Squirrel.

Tommy listened and slowly a smile widened. "Hooty didn't get you, after all!" he muttered. Then in a minute he added: "I'm glad of it. And you haven't anything more to fear from me. You won't believe it, but you haven't. You may be mischievous, but I guess you have troubles enough without me adding to them. Oh, but I'm glad I'm not a squirrel! Being a boy's good enough for me, 'specially 'long 'bout Christmas time. I bet Sis will be tickled with these greens. But it's queer what happens when I sit down on this old rock!"

He frowned at it as if he couldn't understand it at all. Then he gathered up his load of greens, and, with the merriest of whistles, trudged homeward. And to this day Chatterer the Red Squirrel cannot understand how it came about that from that Christmas he and Tommy became fast friends. But they did.

Perhaps the wishing-stone could tell if it would.

III
Why Peter Rabbit Has One Less Enemy

PETER RABBIT was happy. There was no question about that. You had only to watch him a few minutes to know it. He couldn't hide that happiness any more than the sun at midday can hide when there are no clouds in the sky. Happiness seemed to fairly shoot from his long heels as they twinkled merrily this way and that way through the brier-patch. Peter was doing crazy things. He was so happy that he was foolish. Happiness, you know, is the only excuse for foolishness. And Peter was foolish, very, very foolish. He would suddenly jump into the air, kick his long heels, dart off to one side, change his mind and dart the other way, run in a circle, and then abruptly plump himself down under a bush and sit as still as if he couldn't move. Then, without any warning at all, he would cut up some other funny antic.

He was so foolish and so funny that finally Tommy, who, unseen by Peter, was watching him, laughed aloud. Perhaps Peter doesn't like being laughed at. Most people don't. It may be Peter was a little bit uncertain as to why he was being laughed at. Anyway, with a sudden thump of his stout hind-legs, he scampered out of sight along one of his private little

36

paths which led into the very thickest tangle in the old brier-patch.

"I'll have to come over here with my gun and get that rabbit for my dinner," said Tommy, as he trudged homeward. "Probably though, if I have a gun, I won't see him at all. It's funny how a fellow is forever seeing things when he hasn't got a gun, and when he goes hunting he never sees anything!"

Tommy had come to the great gray stone which was his favorite resting-place. He sat down from sheer force of habit. Somehow, he never could get past that stone without sitting down on it for a few minutes. It seemed to just beg to be sat on. He was still thinking of Peter Rabbit.

"I wonder what made him feel so frisky," thought Tommy. Then he laughed aloud once more as he remembered how comical Peter had looked. It must be fun to feel as happy as all that. Without once thinking of where he was, Tommy exclaimed aloud: "I declare, I wish I were a rabbit!"

He was. His wish had come true. Just as quick as that, he found himself a rabbit. You see, he had been sitting on the wishing-stone. If he had remembered, perhaps, he wouldn't have wished. But he had forgotten, and now here he was, looking as if he might very well be own brother to Peter Rabbit. Not only did he look like Peter, but he felt like him. Anyway, he felt a crazy impulse to run and jump and do foolish things, and he did them. He just couldn't help doing them. It was his way of showing how good he felt, just as shouting is a boy's way, and singing is the way of a bird.

But in the very midst of one of his wildest whirls, he heard a sound that brought him up short, as still as a stone. It was the sound of a heavy thump, and it came from the direction of the brier-patch. Tommy didn't need to be told that it was a signal, a signal from Peter Rabbit to all other rabbits within hearing distance. He didn't know just the meaning of that signal, and, because he didn't, he just sat still. Now it happens that that was exactly what that signal meant—to sit tight and not move. Peter had seen something that to him looked very suspicious. So on general principles he had signaled, and then had himself sat perfectly still until he should discover if there was any real danger.

Now Tommy didn't know this, but being a rabbit now, he felt as a rabbit feels, and, from the second he heard that thump, he was as frightened as he had been happy a minute before. And being frightened, yet not knowing of what he was afraid, he sat absolutely still, listening with all his might, and looking this way and that, as best he could, without moving his head. And all the time, he worked his nose up and down, up and down, as all rabbits do, and tested the air for strange smells.

Presently Tommy heard behind him a sound that filled him with terrible fear. It was a loud sniff, sniff. Rolling his eyes back so that he could look behind without turning his head, he saw a dog sniffing and snuffing in the grass. Now that dog wasn't very big as dogs go, but he was so much bigger than even the largest rabbit, that to Tommy he looked like a giant. The terrible fear that filled him clutched at Tommy's heart until it seemed as if it would stop beating. What should he do, sit still or run? Somehow he was afraid to do either. Just then the matter was settled for him. "*Thump, thump, thump!*" the signal came along the ground from the brier-patch, and almost any one would have known just by the short sharp sound that those thumps meant "Run!" At just the same instant, the dog caught the scent of Tommy full and strong. With a roar of his great voice he sprang forward, his nose in Tommy's tracks.

Tommy waited no longer. With a great bound he leaped forward in the direction of the brier-patch. How he did run! A dozen bounds brought him to the brier-patch, and there just before him was a tiny path under the brambles. He didn't stop to question how it came there or who had made it. He dodged in and scurried along it to the very middle of the brier-patch. Then he stopped to listen and look. The dog had just reached the edge of the briers. He knew where Tommy had gone. Of course he knew. His nose told him that. He thrust his head in at the entrance to the little path and tried to crawl in. But the sly old brambles tore his long tender ears, and he yelped with pain now instead of with the excitement of the chase. Then he backed out, whining and yelping. He ran around the edge of the brier-patch looking for some place where he could get in more comfortably. But there was no place, and after a while he gave up and went off.

Tommy sat right where he was until he was quite sure that the dog had gone. When he *was* quite sure, he started to explore the brier-patch, for he was very curious to see what it was like in there. He found little paths leading in all directions. Some of them led right through the very thickest tangles of ugly looking brambles, and Tommy found that he could run along these with never a fear of a single scratch. And as he hopped along, he knew that here he was safe, absolutely safe from most of his enemies, for no one bigger than he could possibly get through those briers without being terribly scratched.

So it was with a very comfortable feeling that Tommy peered out through the brambles and watched that annoying dog trot off in disgust. He felt that never, so long as he was within running distance of the brier-patch, would he be afraid of a dog. Right into the midst of his pleasant thoughts broke a rude *"Thump, thump, thump!"* It wasn't a danger-signal this time. That is, it didn't mean "Run for your life." Tommy was very sure of that. And yet it might be a kind of danger-signal, too. It all depended on what Tommy decided to do. There it was again—*"Thump, thump, thump!"* It had an ugly, threatening sound. Tommy knew just as well as if there had been spoken words instead of more thumps on the ground that he was being warned to get out of the brier-patch—that he had no right there, because it belonged to some one else.

But Tommy had no intention of leaving such a fine place, such a beautifully safe place, unless he had to, and no mere thumps on the ground could make him believe that. He could thump himself. He did. Those long hind-legs of his were just made for thumping. When he hit the ground with them, he did it with a will, and the thumps he made sounded just as ugly and threatening as the other fellow's, and he knew that the other fellow knew exactly what they meant—"I'll do as I please! Put me out if you can!"

It was very clear that this was just what the other proposed to do if his thumps meant anything at all. Presently Tommy saw a trim, neat-looking rabbit in a little open space, and it was something of a relief to find that he was about Tommy's own size. "If I can't whip him, he certainly can't whip me," thought Tommy, and straightway thumped, "I'm coming," in reply to the stranger's angry demand that he come out and fight.

Now the stranger was none other than Peter Rabbit, and he was very indignant. He considered that he owned the brier-patch. He was perfectly willing that any other rabbit should find safety there in time of danger, but when the danger was past, they must get out. Tommy hadn't; therefore he must be driven out.

Peter Rabbit was very indignant. *Page 41.*

Now if Tommy had been himself, instead of a rabbit, never, never would he have dreamed of fighting as he was preparing to fight now—by biting and kicking, particularly kicking. But for a rabbit, kicking was quite the correct and proper thing. In fact, it was the only way to fight. So instead of coming together head-on, Tommy and Peter approached each other in queer little half-side-wise rushes, each watching for a chance to use his stout hind-legs. Suddenly Peter rushed, jumped, and—well, when Tommy picked himself up, he felt very much as a boy feels when he has been tackled and thrown in a foot-ball game. Certainly Peter's hind-legs were in good working order.

Just a minute later Tommy's chance came, and Peter was sent sprawling. Like a flash, Tommy was after him, biting and pulling out little bunches of soft fur. So they fought until at last they were so out of wind and so tired that there was no fight left in either. Then they lay and panted for breath, and quite suddenly they forgot their quarrel. Each knew that he couldn't whip the other; and, that being so, what was the use of fighting?

"I suppose the brier-patch is big enough for both of us," said Peter, after a little.

"I'll live on one side, and you live on the other," replied Tommy. And so it was agreed.

In three things, Tommy found that, as a rabbit, he was not unlike Tommy the boy. These three were appetite, curiosity, and a decided preference for pleasure rather than labor. Tommy felt as if he lived to eat instead of eating to live. He wanted to eat most of the time. It seemed as if he never could get his stomach really full. There was one satisfaction, and that was that he never had to look very far for something to eat. There were clover and grass just outside the brier-patch,—all he wanted for the taking. There were certain tender-leaved plants for a change, not to mention tender bark from young trees and bushes. With Peter he made occasional visits to a not too distant garden, where they fairly reveled in goodies.

These visits were in the nature of adventure. It seemed to Tommy that not even Danny Meadow-Mouse had so many enemies as he and Peter had. They used to talk it over sometimes. "It isn't fair," said Peter, in a grieved tone. "We don't hurt anybody. We don't do the least bit of harm to any one, and yet it isn't safe for us to play two minutes outside the brier-patch without keeping watch. No, sir, it isn't fair! There's Redtail the Hawk watching this very minute from way up there in the sky. He looks as if he were just sailing round and round for the fun of it; but he isn't. He's just watching for you or me to get one too many jumps away from these old briers. Then down he'll come like a shot. Now what harm have we ever done Redtail or any of his family? Tell me that."

With Peter he made visits to a garden. *Page 44.*

Of course Tommy couldn't tell him that, and so Peter went on: "When I was a baby, I came very near to finding out just how far it is from Mr. Blacksnake's mouth to his stomach by the inside passage, and all that saved me was the interference of a boy, who set me free. Now that I'm grown, I'm not afraid of Mr. Blacksnake,—though I keep out of his way,—but I have to keep on the watch all the time for that boy!"

"The same one?" asked Tommy.

"The very same!" replied Peter. "He's forever setting his dog after me and trying to get a shot at me with his terrible gun. Yet I've never done *him* any harm,—nor the dog either."

"It's very curious," said Tommy, not knowing what else to say.

"It seems to me there ought to be some time when it is reasonably safe for an honest rabbit to go abroad," continued Peter, who, now that he was started, seemed bound to make the worst of his troubles. "At night, I cannot even dance in the moonlight without all the time looking one way for Reddy Fox and another for Hooty the Owl."

"It's a good thing that the brier-patch is always safe," said Tommy, because he could think of nothing else to say.

"But it isn't!" snapped Peter. "I wish to goodness it was! Now there's—listen!" Peter sat very still with his ears pricked forward. Something very like a look of fear grew and grew in his eyes. Tommy sat quite as still and listened with all his might. Presently he heard a faint rustling. It sounded as if it was in one of the little paths through the brier-patch. Yes, it surely was, and it was drawing nearer. Tommy gathered himself together for instant flight, and a strange fear gripped his heart.

"It's Billy Mink!" gasped Peter. "If he follows you, don't run into a hole in the ground, or into a hollow log, whatever you do! Keep going! He'll get tired after a while. There he is—run!"

Peter bounded off one way and Tommy another. After a few jumps, Tommy squatted to make sure whether or not he was being followed. He saw a slim, dark form slipping through the brambles, and he knew that Billy Mink was following Peter. Tommy couldn't help a tiny sigh of relief. He was sorry for Peter; but Peter knew every path and twist and turn, while he didn't. It was a great deal better that Peter should be the one to try to fool Billy Mink.

So Tommy sat perfectly still and watched. He saw Peter twist and turn, run in a circle, crisscross, run back on his own trail, and make a break by leaping far to one side. He saw Billy Mink follow every twist and turn, his nose in Peter's tracks. When he reached the place where Peter had broken the trail, he ran in ever widening circles until he picked it up again, and once more Peter was on the run. Tommy felt little cold shivers chase up and down his back as he watched how surely and persistently Billy Mink followed. And then—he hardly knew how it happened—Peter had jumped right over him, and there was Billy Mink coming! There was nothing to do but run, and Tommy ran. He doubled and twisted and played all the tricks he had seen Peter play, and then at last, when he was beginning to get quite tired, he played the same trick on Peter that had seemed so dreadful when Peter played it on him; he led Billy Mink straight to where Peter was sitting, and once more Peter was the hunted.

But Billy Mink was getting tired. After a little, he gave up and went in quest of something more easily caught.

Peter came back to where Tommy was sitting.

"Billy Mink's a tough customer to get rid of alone, but, with some one to change off with, it is no trick at all!" said he. "It wouldn't work so well with his cousin, Shadow the Weasel. He's the one I *am* afraid of. I think we should be safer if we had some new paths; what do you think?"

Tommy confessed that he thought so too. It would have been very much easier to have dodged Billy Mink if there had been a few more cross paths. "We'd better make them before we need them more than we did this time," said Peter; and, as this was just plain, sound, rabbit common sense, Tommy was forced to agree. And so it was that he learned that a rabbit must work if he would live long and be happy. He didn't think of it in just this way as he patiently cut paths through the brambles and tangles of bush and vine. It was fear, just plain fear, that was driving him. And even this drove him to work only by spells. Between times, when he wasn't eating, he sat squatting under a bush just lazily dreaming, but always ready to run for his life.

In the moonlight he and Peter loved to gambol and play in some open space where there was room to jump and dance; but, even in the midst of these joyous times, they must need sit up every minute or so to stop, look, and listen for danger. It was at night, too, that they wandered farthest from the brier-patch. Once they met Bobby Coon, and Peter warned Tommy never to allow Bobby to get him cornered. And once they met Jimmy Skunk, who paid no attention to them at all, but went right on about his business. It was hard to believe that he was another to be warned against; but so Peter said, and Peter ought to know if anybody did.

So Tommy learned to be ever on the watch. He learned to take note of his neighbors. He could tell by the sound of his voice when Sammy Jay was watching Reddy Fox, and when he saw a hunter. When Blacky the Crow was on guard, he knew that he was reasonably safe from surprise. At least once a day, but more often several times a day, he had a narrow escape. But he grew used to it, and, as soon as a fright was over, he forgot it. It was the only way to do.

As he learned more and more how to watch, and to care for himself, he grew bolder. Curiosity led him farther and farther from the brier-patch. And then,

Once they met Bobby Coon. *Page 49.*

one day, he discovered that Reddy Fox was between him and his castle. There was nothing for it but to run and twist and double and dodge. Every trick he had learned he tried in vain. He was in the open, and Reddy was too wise to be fooled. He was right at Tommy's heels now, and with every jump Tommy expected to feel those cruel white teeth. Just ahead was a great rock. If he could reach that, perhaps there might be a crack in it big enough for a frightened little rabbit to squeeze into, or a hole under it where he might find safety.

He was almost up to it. Would he be able to make it? One jump! He could hear Reddy panting. Two jumps! He could feel Reddy's breath. Three jumps! He was on the rock! and—slowly Tommy rubbed his eyes. Reddy Fox was nowhere to be seen. Of course not! No fox would be foolish enough to come near a *boy* sitting in plain sight. Tommy looked over to the old brier-patch. That at least was real. Slowly he walked over to it. Peering under the bushes, he saw Peter Rabbit squatting perfectly still, yet ready to run.

"You don't need to, Peter," said he. "You don't need to. You can cut one boy off that long list of enemies you are always watching for. You see, I know just how you feel, Peter!"

He walked around to the other side of the brier-patch, and, stooping down, thumped the ground once with his hand. There was an answering thump

Reddy Fox was between him and his castle. *Page 51.*

from the spot where he had seen Peter Rabbit. Tommy smiled.

"We're friends, Peter," said he, "and it's all on account of the wishing-stone. I'll never hunt you again. My! I wouldn't be a rabbit for anything in the world. Being a boy is good enough for me!"

IV
How It Happened that Reddy Fox
Gained a Friend

IT was funny that Tommy never could pass that great gray stone without sitting down on it for a few minutes. It seemed as if he just couldn't, that was all. It had been a favorite seat ever since he was big enough to drive the cows to pasture and go after them at night. It was just far enough from home for him to think that he needed a rest when he reached it. You know a growing boy needs to rest often— except when he is playing. He used to take all his troubles there to think them over. The queer part of it is he left a great many of them there, though he didn't seem to know it. If Tommy ever could have seen in one pile all the troubles he had left at that old gray stone, I am afraid that he would have called it the trouble-stone instead of the wishing-stone.

It was only lately that he had begun to call it the wishing-stone. Several times when he had been sitting on it, he had wished foolish wishes and they had come true. At least, it seemed as if they had come true. They had come as true as he ever wanted them to. He was thinking something of this kind now as he stood idly kicking at the old stone. Presently he stopped kicking at it, and, from force of habit, sat down on it. It was a bright, sunshiny day, one of those warm days that sometimes happen right in the middle of winter, as if the weather-man had somehow got mixed and slipped a spring day into the wrong place in the calendar.

From where he sat, Tommy could look over to the Green Forest, which was green now only where the pine-trees and the hemlock-trees and the spruce-trees grew. All the rest was bare and brown, save that the ground was white with snow. He could look across the white meadow-land to the Old Pasture, where in places the brush was so thick that, in summer, he sometimes had to hunt to find the cows. Now, even from this distance, he could trace the windings of the cow-paths, each a ribbon of spotless white. It puzzled him at first. He scowled at them.

"When the whole thing is covered with snow, it ought to be harder to see those paths, but instead of that it is easier," he muttered. "'Tain't reasonable!" Tommy never *could* see any sense in grammar. He scowled harder than ever, but the scowl wasn't an unpleasant one. You know there is a difference in scowls. Some are black and heavy, like ugly thunder-heads, and from them flashes of anger are likely to dart any minute, just as the lightning darts out from the thunder-heads. Others are like the big fleecy clouds that hide the sun for a minute or two, and make it seem all the brighter by their passing. There are scowls of anger and scowls of perplexity. It was a scowl of the latter kind that wrinkled Tommy's

forehead now. He was trying to understand something that seemed to him quite as much beyond
common sense as the rules of the grammar he so
detested.

"'Tain't reasonable!" he repeated. "I hadn't ought
to be able to see 'em at all. But I do. They stick out
like—"

No one will ever know just what they stuck out
like, for Tommy never finished that sentence. The
scowl cleared and his freckled face fairly beamed.
He had made a discovery all by himself, and he felt
all the joy of a discoverer. Perhaps you will think it
wasn't much, but it was really important, so far as it
concerned Tommy, because it proved that Tommy
was learning to use his eyes and to understand what
he saw. He had reasoned the thing out, and when
anybody does that, it is always important.

"Why, how simple!" exclaimed Tommy. "Of course
I can see those old paths! It would be funny if I
couldn't. The bushes break through the snow on all
sides, but where the paths are, there is nothing to
break through, and so they are perfectly smooth and
stand right out. Queer I never noticed that before.
Hello! what's that?"

His sharp eyes had caught sight of a little spot of
red up in the Old Pasture. It was moving, and, as he
watched it, it gradually took shape. It was Reddy
Fox, trotting along one of those little white paths.
Apparently, Reddy was going to keep an engagement
somewhere, for he trotted along quite as if he were

bound for some particular place and had no time to waste.

"He's headed this way, and, if I keep still, perhaps he'll come close," thought Tommy.

So he sat as still as if he were part of the old wishing-stone itself. Reddy Fox came straight on. At the edge of the Old Pasture he stopped for a minute and looked across to the Green Forest, as if to make sure that it was perfectly safe to cross the open meadows. Evidently he thought it was, for he resumed his steady trot. If he kept on the way he was headed, he would pass very near to the wishing-stone and to Tommy. Just as he was half-way across the meadows, Chanticleer, Tommy's prize Plymouth Rock rooster, crowed over in the farm-yard. Instantly Reddy stopped with one black paw uplifted and turned his head in the direction of the sound. Tommy could imagine the hungry look in that sharp, crafty face. But Reddy was far too wise to think of going up to the farm-yard in broad daylight, and in a moment resumed his journey.

Nearer and nearer he came, until he was passing not thirty feet away. How handsome he was! His beautiful red coat looked as if the coldest wind never could get through it. His great plume of a tail, black toward the end and just tipped with white, was held high to keep it out of the snow. His black stockings, white vest, and black-tipped ears gave him a wonderfully fine appearance. Quite a dandy is Reddy Fox, and he looked it.

He was almost past, when Tommy squeaked like a mouse. Like a flash Reddy turned, his sharp ears cocked forward, his yellow eyes agleam with hunger. There he stood, as motionless as Tommy himself, eagerness written in every line of his face. It was very clear that, no matter how important his business in the Green Forest was, he didn't intend knowingly to pass anything so delicious as a meadow-mouse. Once more Tommy squeaked. Instantly Reddy took several steps toward him, looking and listening intently. A look of doubt crept into his eager face. That old gray stone didn't look just as he remembered it. For a long minute he stared straight at Tommy. Then a puff of wind fluttered the bottom of Tommy's coat, and perhaps at the same time it carried to Reddy that dreaded man smell.

Reddy almost turned a back-somersault in his hurry to get away. Then he ran. How he did run! In almost no time at all he had reached the Green Forest and vanished from Tommy's sight. Quite without knowing it Tommy sighed.

"My, how handsome he is!" You know Tommy is freckle-faced and rather homely. "And gee, how he can run!" he added admiringly. "It must be fun to be able to run like that. It must be fun to be a fox anyhow. I wonder what it feels like. I wish I were a fox."

If he had remembered where he was, perhaps Tommy would have thought twice before wishing. But he had forgotten. Forgetting was one of Tommy's besetting sins. Hardly had the words left

Then he ran. How he did run! *Page 58.*

his mouth, when Tommy found that he *was* a fox, red-coated, black-stockinged—the very image of Reddy himself. And with that change in himself everything else had changed. It was summer. The Green Meadows and the Green Forest were very beautiful. Even the Old Pasture was beautiful. But Tommy had no eyes for beauty. All that beauty meant nothing to him save that now there was plenty to eat and no great trouble to get it. Everywhere the birds were singing, but, if Tommy heeded at all, it was only to wish that some of the sweet songsters would come down on the ground where he could catch them. Those songs made him hungry. He knew of nothing he liked better, next to fat meadow-mice, than birds. That reminded him that some of them nest on the ground, Mrs. Grouse for instance. He had little hope that he could catch her, for it seemed as if she had eyes in the back of her head; but she should have a family by this time, and if he could find those youngsters—the very thought made his mouth water, and he started for the Green Forest.

Once there, he visited one place after another where he thought he might find Mrs. Grouse. He was almost ready to give up and go back to the Green Meadows to hunt for meadow-mice, when a sudden rustling in the dead leaves made him stop short and strain his ears. There was a faint *kwitt,* and then all was still. Tommy took three or four steps and then—could he believe his eyes? There was Mrs. Grouse fluttering on the ground just in front of

Tommy took three or four steps and then—
could he believe his eyes! *Page 60.*

him! One wing dragged as if broken. Tommy made a quick spring and then another. Somehow Mrs. Grouse just managed to get out of his way. But she couldn't fly. She couldn't run as she usually did. It was only luck that she had managed to evade him. Very stealthily he approached her as she lay fluttering among the leaves. Then, gathering himself for a long jump, he sprang. Once more he missed her, by a mere matter of inches it seemed. The same thing happened again and still again. It was maddening to have such a good dinner so near and yet not be able to get it. Then something happened that made Tommy feel so foolish that he wanted to sneak away. With a roar of wings Mrs. Grouse sailed up over the tree-tops and out of sight!

"Huh! Haven't you learned that trick yet?" said a voice.

Tommy turned. There was Reddy Fox grinning at him. "What trick?" he demanded.

"Why, that old Grouse was just fooling you!" replied Reddy. "There was nothing the matter with her. She was just pretending. She had a whole family of young ones hidden close by the place where you first saw her. My, but you are easy!"

"Let's go right back there!" cried Tommy.

"No use. Not the least bit," declared Reddy. "It's too late. Let's go over on the meadows and hunt for mice."

Together they trotted over to the Green Meadows. All through the grass were private little paths made by the mice. The grass hung over them so that they were more like tunnels than paths. Reddy crouched down by one which smelled very strong of mouse. Tommy crouched down by another. Presently there was the faint sound of tiny feet running. The grass moved ever so little over the small path Reddy was watching. Suddenly he sprang, and his two black paws came down together on something that gave a pitiful squeak. Reddy had caught a mouse without even seeing it. He had known just where to jump by the movement of the grass. Presently Tommy caught one the same way. Then, because they knew that the mice right around there were frightened, they moved on to another part of the meadows.

"I know where there are some young wood-chucks," said Tommy, who had unsuccessfully tried for one of them that very morning.

"Where?" demanded Reddy.

"Over by that old tree on the edge of the meadow," replied Tommy. "It isn't the least bit of use to try for them. They don't go far enough away from their hole, and their mother keeps watch all the time. There she is now."

Sure enough, there sat old Mrs. Chuck, looking, at that distance, for all the world like a stake driven in the ground.

"Come on," said Reddy. "We'll have one of those chucks."

But instead of going toward the woodchuck home, Reddy turned in quite the opposite direction.

"Come on," said Reddy. "We'll have one
of those chucks." *Page 63.*

Tommy didn't know what to make of it, but he said nothing, and trotted along behind. When they were where Reddy knew that Mrs. Chuck could no longer see them, he stopped.

"There's no hurry," said he. "There seems to be plenty of grasshoppers here, and we may as well catch a few. When Mrs. Chuck has forgotten all about us, we'll go over there."

Tommy grinned to himself. "If he thinks we are going to get over there without being seen, he's got something to learn," thought Tommy. But he said nothing, and, for lack of anything better to do, he caught grasshoppers. After a while, Reddy said he guessed it was about time to go chuck-hunting.

"You go straight over there," said he. "When you get near, Mrs. Chuck will send all the little Chucks down into their hole and then she will follow, only she'll stay where she can peep out and watch you. Go right up to the hole so that she will go down out of sight and wait there until I come. I'll hide right back of that tree, and then you go off as if you had given up trying to catch any of them. Go hunt meadow-mice far enough away so that she won't be afraid. I'll do the rest."

Tommy didn't quite see through the plan, but he did as he was told. As he drew near Mrs. Chuck, she did just as Reddy said she would—sent her youngsters down underground. Then, as he drew nearer, she followed them. Tommy kept on right up to her doorstep. The smell of those Chucks was maddening. He was tempted to try to dig them out, only somehow he just felt that it would be of no use. He was still half minded to try, however, when Reddy came trotting up and flattened himself in the long grass behind the trunk of the tree. Tommy knew then that it was time for him to do the rest of his part. He turned his back on the woodchuck home and trotted off across the meadow. He hadn't gone far when, looking back, he saw Mrs. Chuck sitting up very straight and still on her doorstep, watching him. Not once did she take her eyes from him. Tommy kept on, and presently began to hunt for meadow-mice. But he kept one eye on Mrs. Chuck, and presently he saw her look this way and that, as if to make sure that all was well. Then she must have told her children that they could come out to play once more, for out they came. By this time Tommy was so excited that he almost forgot that he was supposed to be hunting mice.

Presently he saw a red flash from behind the old tree. There was a frightened scurry of little Chucks and old Mrs. Chuck dove into her hole. Reddy barked joyfully. Tommy hurried to join him. There on the ground lay two little Chucks with the life shaken out of them.

"Didn't I tell you we'd have Chuck for dinner?" said Reddy. "What one can't do, two can."

After that, Tommy and Reddy often hunted together, and Reddy taught Tommy many things. So the summer passed with plenty to eat and nothing to worry about. Not once had he known that terrible fear—the fear of being hunted—which is so large a part of the lives of Danny Meadow Mouse and Peter Rabbit, and even Chatterer the Red Squirrel. Instead of being afraid, he was feared. He was the hunter instead of the hunted. Day and night, for he was abroad at night quite as much as by day, he went where he pleased and did as he pleased, and was happy, for there was nothing to worry him. Having plenty to eat, he kept away from the homes of men. He had been warned that there was danger there.

At last the weather grew cold. There were no more grasshoppers. There were no more foolish young rabbits or woodchucks or grouse, for those who had escaped had grown up and were wise and smart. Every day it grew harder to get enough to eat. The cold weather made him hungrier than ever, and now he had little time for sun-naps or idle play. He had to spend most of the time that he was awake hunting. He never knew where the next meal was coming from, as did thrifty Striped Chipmunk, and Happy Jack Squirrel, and Danny Meadow Mouse. It was hunt, hunt, hunt, and a meal only when his wits were sharper than the wits of those he hunted. He knew now what real hunger was. He knew what it was most of the time. So when, late one after-noon, he surprised a fat hen who had strayed away from the flock behind the barn of a lonely farm, he thought that never had he tasted anything more delicious. Thereafter he visited chicken-houses and

He surprised a fat hen who had strayed
away from the flock. *Page 67.*

stole many fat pullets. To him they were no more than the wild birds he hunted, only more foolish and so easily caught.

And then one morning after a successful raid on a poultry-house, he heard for the first time the voices of dogs on his trail. He, the hunter, was being hunted. At first it didn't bother him at all. He would run away and leave them far behind. So he ran, and when their voices were faint and far away, he lay down to rest. But presently he grew uneasy. Those voices were drawing nearer. Those dogs were following his every twist and turn with their noses in his tracks, just as he had so often followed a rabbit. For hours he ran, and still those dogs followed. He was almost ready to drop, when he chanced to run along in a tiny brook, and, after he left that, he heard no more of the dogs that day. So he learned that running water broke his trail.

The next day the dogs found his trail again, and, as he ran from them through a swamp, there was a sudden flash and a dreadful noise. Something stung him sharply on the shoulder. As he looked back, he caught a glimpse of a man with something in his hands that looked like a stick with smoke coming from the end of it. That night, as he lay licking his wounds, he knew that now he, who had known no fear, would never again be free from it—the fear of man.

Little by little he learned how to fool and outwit the dogs. He learned that water destroyed his scent.

He learned that dry sand did not hold it. He learned to run along stone walls and then jump far out into the field and so break his trail. He learned that, if he dashed through a flock of sheep, the foolish animals would rush around in aimless fright, and their feet would stamp out his trail. These and many other sharp tricks he learned, so that after a while he had no fear of the dogs. But his fear of man grew greater rather than less, and was with him at all times.

So all through the fall he hunted and was hunted. Then came the snow, the beautiful white snow. All day it fell, and when at night the moon came out, the earth was covered with a wonderful white carpet. Through the Green Forest and over the meadows Tommy hunted. One long shivering little wood-mouse he dug out of a moldering old stump, but this was only a bite. He visited one hen-house after another, only to find each without so much as a loose board by means of which he might get in. It was dreadful to be so hungry.

As if this were not enough, the breaking of the day brought the sound of dogs on his trail. "I'll fool them in short order," thought he.

Alas! Running in the snow was a very different matter from running on the bare ground. One trick after another he tried, the very best he knew, the ones which never had failed before; but all in vain. Wherever he stepped he left a footprint plain to see. Though he might fool the noses of the dogs, he could not fool the eyes of their masters. Now one thing he had long ago learned, and this was never to seek his underground den unless he must, for then the dogs and the hunters would know where he lived. So now Tommy ran and ran, hoping to fool the dogs, but not able to. At last he realized this, and started for his den. He felt that he had got to. Running in the snow was hard work. His legs ached with weariness. His great plume of a tail, of which he was so proud, was a burden now. It had become wet with the snow and so heavy that it hampered and tired him.

A great fear, a terrible fear, filled Tommy's heart. Would he be able to reach that snug den in time? He was panting hard for breath, and his legs moved slower and slower. The voices of the dogs seemed to be in his very ears. Glancing back over his shoulder, he could see them gaining with every jump, the fierce joy of the hunt and the lust of killing in their eyes. He knew now the feeling, the terror and dreadful hopelessness, of the meadow-mice and rabbits he had so often run down. Just ahead was a great gray rock. From it he would make one last long jump in an effort to break the trail. In his fear he quite forgot that he was in plain sight now, and that his effort would be useless.

Up on the rock he leaped wearily, and—Tommy rubbed his eyes. Then he pinched himself to make quite sure that he was really himself. He shivered, for he was in a cold sweat—the sweat of fear. Before him stretched the snow-covered meadows, and away over beyond was the Old Pasture with the cow-paths showing like white ribbons. Half-way across the meadows, running toward him with their noses to the ground and making the echoes ring with the joy of the hunt, were two hounds. A dark figure moving on the edge of the Old Pasture caught his eyes and held them. It was a hunter. Reddy Fox, handsome, crafty Reddy, into whose hungry yellow eyes he had looked so short a time before, would soon be running for his life.

Hastily Tommy jumped to his feet and hurried over to the trail Reddy had made as he ran for the Green Forest. With eager feet he kicked the snow over those telltale tracks for a little way. He waited for those eager hounds, and when they reached the place where he had broken the trail, he drove them away. They and the hunter might pick up the trail again in the Green Forest, but at least Reddy would have time to get a long start of them and a good chance of getting away altogether.

Then he went back to the wishing-stone and looked down at it thoughtfully. "And I actually wished I could be a fox!" he exclaimed. "My, but I'm glad I'm not! I guess Reddy has trouble enough without me making him any more. He may kill a lot of innocent little creatures, but he has to live, and it's no more than men do." (He was thinking of the chicken dinner he would have that day.) "I'm going straight over to the Old Pasture and take up that trap I set yesterday. I guess a boy's troubles don't amount to much, after all. I'm gladder than ever that I'm a boy, and—and—well, if Reddy Fox is smart enough to get one of my chickens now and then, he's welcome. It must be awful to be hungry all the time."

V
How Tommy Envied Honker the Goose

THE feel of spring was in the air. The sound of it filled Tommy's ears. The smell of it filled his nostrils and caused him to take long, deep breaths. The sight of it gladdened his eyes, and the joy of it thrilled his heart. For the spring, you know, has really arrived only when it can be felt, heard, smelled, and seen, and has the power to fill all living things with abounding joy and happiness.

Winter had been long in going. It seemed to Tommy that it never would go. He liked winter. Oh, yes, Tommy liked winter! He liked to skate and slide, to build snow forts and houses, and make snow men. He liked to put on his snowshoes and tramp through the Green Forest, for many are the secrets of the summer which the winter reveals to those with eyes to see, and Tommy was trying to train his eyes to be of that kind. But when it was time for winter to go, he wanted it to go quickly, and it hadn't. It had dragged on and dragged on. To be sure, there had been a few springlike days, but they had been only an aggravation.

But this day was different, and Tommy knew that at last spring had arrived. It was not that it was long past time, for it was now almost April. It was something more. It was just a something that, throbbing all through him, told him that this time there was no mistake—spring was really here. There was a softness in the touch of gentle Sister Southwind which was like a caress. From over in the Green Forest came the gurgle of the Laughing Brook, and mingling with it was the soft whistle of Winsome Bluebird, the cheery song of Welcome Robin, the joyous greeting of Little Friend the Song-sparrow, the clear lilt of Meadow-lark, the sweet love call of Tomtit, the Chickadee, and under all a subdued murmur, sensed rather than really heard, as of a gentle stirring of reawakened life. So Tommy *heard* the spring.

And in each long breath he drew there was the odor of damp, warm soil such as the earth gives up only at this season. And so Tommy *smelled* the spring.

And looking from the top of the hill above the wishing-stone down across the Green Meadows to the Old Pasture and beyond to the Purple Hills, he saw all as through a soft and beautiful haze, which was neither fog nor smoke, but as if old Mother Nature had drawn an exquisite veil over the face of the earth until it should be made beautiful. And so Tommy *saw* the spring.

He whistled joyously as he tramped down to the dear old wishing-stone and sat down on it, his hands clasped about his crossed knees. Seasons came and seasons went, but the wishing-stone, the great, gray

stone which overlooked the Green Meadows, remained always the same. How many, many winters
it must have seen go, and how many, many springs it
must have seen come, some early and some, like this
one, late, but all beautiful! In all the years it had been
there how many of old Mother Nature's children,
little people in fur, little people in feathers, little
people in scaly suits, and little people with neither
fur nor feathers nor scales, but with gauzy or beautifully colored wings, or crawling with many feet,
must have rested there just as he was doing now!

Somehow Tommy always got to thinking of these
little people whenever he sat on the wishing-stone.
From it he had watched many of them and learned
much of their ways. But he had learned still more
by wishing. That seems queer, but it was so. He had
wished that he was a meadow-mouse, and no sooner
had he wished it than he had been one. In turn he
had wished himself into a red squirrel, a rabbit,
and a fox, and he had lived their lives; had learned
how they work and play; how sometimes they have
plenty, but quite as often go hungry, sometimes very
hungry, and how always they are under the shadow
of fear, and the price of life is eternal watchfulness.

"I suppose some people would say that I fell asleep
and dreamed it all, but I know better," said Tommy.
"If they were dreams, why don't I have the same kind
at home in bed? But it's only out here on this old
stone when I wish that I were something that I become it. So of course it isn't a dream! Now I think of

it, every single time I've wished myself one of these little animals, it has been because I thought they had a better and an easier time than I do, and every time I've been mighty glad that I'm just what I am. I wonder—" He paused a minute, for a sudden thought had popped into his head. "I wonder," he finished, "if those wishes came true just to teach me not to be discontented. I wonder if a wish would come true if I weren't discontented!"

He was still wondering when, floating down out of the sky, came a clear *"Honk, honk, honk, k'honk, honk, honk, k'honk."* Instantly Tommy turned his freckled face and eager eyes skyward.

"Wild geese!" he exclaimed.

"Honk, honk, k'honk, honk!" The sound was loud and clear, but it seemed to come from nowhere in particular and everywhere in general. Of course it came from somewhere up in the sky, but it was very hard to place it as from any particular part. It was a good two minutes before Tommy's eyes, sharp as they were, found what he was looking for—a black wedge moving across the sky, a wedge made up of little, black living spots. At least they looked little. That was because they were so high, so very high, in the sky. He knew that each of those black spots was a great, broad-winged bird—a Canada goose. He could see the long outstretched necks as tiny black lines. One behind another in two long lines which met in a letter V, like well-drilled soldiers maintaining perfect formation, the leader at

the apex of the V, and behind him each bird a given distance from the one in front, they moved steadily across the sky, straight into the north.

"Honk, honk, k'honk, honk, k'honk, k'honk, honk!" There was something indescribably thrilling in the sound. It made the blood leap and race through Tommy's veins. Long after the living wedge had passed beyond his vision those clarion notes rang in his ears— *"honk, honk, k'honk, honk, k'honk, k'honk, honk!"* They were at once a challenge and a call to the wild freedom of the great wilderness. They filled his heart with a great longing. It swelled and pulsed with a vast desire.

"Oh, he sighed, it must be great to be able to fly like that. I would rather fly than do anything I know of. I envy old Honker in the lead there, I do. I wish I could join him this very minute!"

Of course that wish had slipped out unthinkingly. But that made no difference. Tommy had wished, and now here he was high in the air, no longer a boy, but a great bird, the last one in a long line of great birds beating the thin air with stout, tireless wings as they followed Honker, the leader, straight into the north. Far, far below lay the Great World. It seemed to Tommy that he had no part in it now. A fierce tumultuous joy surged through him and demanded expression. Spring had come, and he must tell those plodding creatures, mere specks, crawling on the distant earth. *Honk, honk, k'honk, honk, k'honk!*

"It must be great to be able to fly like that." *Page 78*.

Never in all his life had Tommy felt such a thrill as possessed him now. Looking down, he saw brown meadows and pastures showing just a hint of green here and there, green forests and bare wood-lands, silver threads, which he knew to be rivers, shining spots which were lakes and ponds, and villages which looked like toys. Once they passed over a great city, but it did not look great at all. Seen through the murk of the smoke from many factory chimneys, it was not unlike an ant-hill which has been opened,—tiny black objects, which were really men, women, children, horses, and motor-cars, seeming to hurry aimlessly in all directions, for all the world like ants.

So all day they flew, crying the glad message of the spring to the crawling things below. Just a little while before the setting of the sun, Honker, the leader, slanted down toward a shining spot in the heart of a great forest, and the others followed. Rapidly the shining spot grew in size until below them lay a pond far from the homes of men, and to the very middle of this Honker led the way, while from the whole flock broke an excited gabbling, for they had flown far and were tired. With a splash Honker struck the water, and with splash after splash the others followed, Tommy the last, because, you know, he was at the end of one of those long lines.

Then for a while they rested, the wise old leader scanning the shores with keen eyes for possible danger. Satisfied that all was well, he gave a signal

Honker on the watch. *Page 82*.

and led the way to a secluded cove where the water was shallow and the shore marshy. It was clear that he had been there before, and had come with a purpose. Slowly they swam, Honker well in the lead, necks held high, the eyes of all alert and studying the nearing shore. There was no honking now, not a sound. To Tommy, in his inexperience, such watchfulness seemed needless. What possible danger could there be in such a lonely place? But he wisely kept his place and did as the others did. At length they were close to shore, and Honker gave a low signal which meant that all was well. Instantly the formation was broken, and with a low, contented gabbling the flock began feeding on eel-grass, roots, and sedges from the mud at the bottom. For an hour they fed, then they swam about, or sat on the shore preening their feathers while the shadows deepened. But all the time Honker and some of the older ganders with eyes and ears alert were on guard. And when at last Tommy put his head under his wing to sleep, a great content filled his heart.

The next day was much like the first. With break of day they had breakfasted, and then, at a signal from Honker, they had mounted up, up into the blue vault, and all day they had heralded the spring to the earth below as they flew into the north. So it was the next day and the next, wise old Honker leading them to some chosen secluded resting-place each night.

Gradually the face of the earth below changed. There were no more cities. The villages became smaller and farther between, and at last they saw no more, only here and there a lonely farm. Great forests and lakes succeeded each other. The air grew colder, but with his thick coat of feathers Tommy minded it not at all. Then, one day, they found they had outflown the spring. Below them the earth was still frozen and snow-covered. The ponds and lakes were still icebound. Reluctantly Honker turned back to their last stopping-place, and there for a week they rested in peace and security, though not in contentment, for the call of the north, the far north, with its nesting-grounds, was ever with them, and made them impatient and eager to be on their way. The daily flights were shorter now, and there were frequent rests of days at a time, for spring advanced slowly, and they must wait for the unlocking of the lakes and rivers. The forests changed; the trees became low and stunted. At last they came to a vast region of bogs and swamps and marshes around shallow lakes and ponds, a great lonely wilderness, a mighty solitude. At least that is what Tommy would have thought it had he been a boy or a man instead of a smart young gander.

It was neither lonely nor a solitude to him now, but the haven which had been the object of those hundreds of miles of strong-winged flight. It was the nesting-ground. It was home! And how could it be lonely with flock after flock of his own kind coming in every hour of every day; with thousands of ducks pouring in in swift winged flight, and countless smaller birds, all intent on home-building?

The flock broke up into pairs, each intent on speedily securing a home of their own. On the ground they made great nests of small sticks and dead grass with a soft lining of down. In each presently were five big eggs. And soon there were downy goslings—scores and scores of them—in the water with their mothers for the first swimming lesson. Then the old birds had to be more vigilant than before, for there were dangers, many of them, even in that far wilderness: prowling foxes, hungry lynxes, crafty mink, hawks, fierce owls, each watching for the chance to dine on tender young goose. So the summer, short in that far northern region, passed, and the young birds grew until they were as large as their parents, and able to care for themselves.

Cold winds swept down out of the frozen arctic with warning that already winter had begun the southward march. Then began a great gathering of the geese, and a dividing into flocks, each with a chosen leader, chosen for his strength, his wisdom, and his ability to hold his leadership against all comers. Many a battle between ambitious young ganders and old leaders did Tommy witness, but he wisely forbore to challenge old Honker, the leader who had led the way north, and when the latter gathered the flock for the journey he was one of the first to fall in line.

The first swimming lesson. *Page 84.*

A thousand plus a thousand miles and more stretched before them as they turned to the south, but to the strength of their broad wings the distance was as nothing. But this was to be a very different journey from their trip north, as Tommy soon found out. Then they had been urged on day by day by a great longing to reach their destination. Now in place of longing was regret. There was no joy in the going. They were going because they must. They had no choice. Winter had begun its southward march.

The flights were comparatively short, for where food was good they stayed until some subtle sense warned old Honker that it was time to be moving. It was when they had left the wilderness and reached the great farm-lands that they lingered longest. There in the stubble of the grain fields was feed a-plenty, and every morning at dawn, and again every afternoon, an hour or so before sundown, Honker led the way to the fields. During the greater part of the day and all night they rested and slept on the bar of a river, or well out on the bosom of a lake.

It was now that Tommy learned a new respect for the cunning of the wise old leader, and also that terrible fear which comes sooner or later to all wild creatures—the fear of man. Time and again, as they approached their chosen feeding-ground, there would come a sharp signal from Honker, and he would abruptly turn the direction of the flight and lead them to another and much poorer feeding-ground. Yet, look as he would, Tommy could see no cause, no danger. At first Tommy thought it was because other geese seemed to have reached the feeding-ground first. He could see them standing stiffly as if watching the new-comers, near them a harmless little heap of straw. He knew that the feeding was better there, and he wanted to go, but the spirit of obedience was strong within him, and he followed with the rest. Once he voiced his disapproval to another bird as they settled some distance away where it was more work to find the scattered grain.

"Watch!" he replied in a low tone. "There comes a flock led by that young upstart who fought and defeated his old leader the day before we left home. He is leading them straight over there."

Tommy watched. Suddenly from that harmless-looking little heap of straw there sprang two spurts of flame, followed by two sharp reports that struck terror to his heart. Even as he beat his way into the air, he looked and saw that foolish young leader and three of his flock falling, stricken and helpless, to the earth, and a man leap from under the straw to pick them up. Then he understood, and a new loyalty to old Honker grew in his heart.

But in spite of the ever-present danger, Honker kept his flock there, for food was good and plentiful, and he had faith in himself, and his flock had faith in him. So they lingered, until a driving snow squall warned them that they must be moving. Keeping just ahead of the on-coming winter, they journeyed

"Watch!" he replied in a low tone. *Page 87.*

south, and at every stopping-place they found men and guns waiting. There was no little pond so lonely but that death might be lurking there. Sometimes the call of their own kind would come up to them. Looking down, they would see geese swimming in seeming security and calling to them to come down and join them. More than once Honker set his wings to accept the invitation, only to once more beat his way upward as his keen eyes detected something amiss on the shore. And so Tommy learned the baseness of man who would use his own kind to decoy them to death.

Came at last a sudden swift advance of cold weather which forced them to fly all night. When day broke, they were weary of wing, and, worse, the air was thick with driving snow. For the first time, Tommy beheld Honker uncertain. He still led the flock, but he led he knew not where, for in the driving snow none could see. Low they flew now, but a little way above the earth, making little progress against the driving storm, and so weary of wing that it was all they could do to keep their heavy bodies up. It was then that the welcome honk of other geese came up to them, and, heading in the direction of the calling voices and honking back their distress, they discovered water below, and gladly, oh, so gladly, set their wings and dropped down into this haven of refuge. Hardly had the first ones hit the water when, bang! bang! bang! bang! the fateful guns roared, and when, out of the confusion into which they were thrown, they once more gathered behind their old leader far out in the middle of the pond, some of the flock were missing.

In clear weather they flew high, and it happened on such a day that, as Tommy looked down, there stirred within him a strange feeling. Below stretched a green forest with broad meadows beyond, and farther still an old brush-grown pasture. Somehow it was wonderfully familiar. Eagerly he looked. There should be something more. Ah, there it was—an old gray boulder overlooking the meadows! Like a magnet, it seemed to draw Tommy down to itself. *"Honk, honk, honk, k'honk!"* Tommy heard the call of his old leader faintly, as if from a distance.

"Honk, honk, honk, k'honk, honk, k'honk, honk!" Tommy opened his eyes and rubbed them confusedly. Where was he? *"Honk, honk, honk, k'honk, honk, k'honk!"* He looked up. There, high in the blue sky, was a living wedge pointing straight into the north, and the joy of the spring was in the wild clamor that came down to him. Slowly he rose from the old wishing-stone, and, with his hands thrust in his pockets, watched the flock until it was swallowed up in the distant haze. Long he stood gazing through unseeing eyes while the wild notes still came to him faintly, and the joy of them rang in his heart. But there was no longing there now, only a vast content.

"It must be great to fly like that!" he murmured. "It must be great, but—" He drew a long breath as he looked over the meadows to the Old Pasture and heard and saw and felt the joy of the spring— "this is good enough for me!" he finished. "I don't envy that old leader a bit. It may be glorious to be wild and free, to look down and see the great world, and all that, but it's more glorious to be safe and carefree, and—and just a boy. No, I don't envy old Honker a little bit. But isn't he wonderful! I—I don't see what men want to hunt him for and try to kill him. They wouldn't if they knew how wonderful he is. I never will. No, sir. I never will! I know how it feels to be hunted, and—and it's dreadful. That's what it is—dreadful! I know! And it's all because of the old wishing-stone. I'm glad I know, and—and— gee, I'm glad it's spring!"

"Honk, honk, honk, k'honk, honk, k'honk!" Another flock of geese were passing over, and Tommy knew that they, too, were glad, oh, so glad, that it was spring!

VI
Tommy Becomes a Very Humble Person

HELLO, old Mr. Sobersides! Where are you bound for?" As he spoke, Tommy thrust a foot in front of old Mr. Toad and laughed as Mr. Toad hopped up on it and then off, quite as if he were accustomed to having big feet thrust in his way. Not that Tommy had especially big feet. They simply were big in comparison with Mr. Toad. "Never saw you in a hurry before," continued Tommy. "What's it all about? You are going as if you were bound for somewhere in particular, and as if you had something special on your mind. What is it, anyway?"

Now of course old Mr. Toad didn't make any reply. At least he didn't make any that Tommy heard. If he had, Tommy wouldn't have understood it. The fact is, it did look, for all the world, as if it was just as Tommy had said. If ever any one had an important engagement to keep and meant to keep it, Mr. Toad did, if looks counted anything. Hoppity-hop-hop-hop, hoppity-hop-hop-hop, he went straight down toward the Green Meadows, and he didn't pay any attention to anybody or anything.

Tommy was interested. He had known old Mr. Toad ever since he could remember, and he couldn't recall ever having seen him go anywhere in particular.

Whenever Tommy had noticed him, he had seemed to be hopping about in the most aimless sort of way, and never took more than a half dozen hops without sitting down to think it over. So it was very surprising to see him traveling along in this determined fashion, and, having nothing better to do, Tommy decided to follow him and find out what he could.

So down the Lone Little Path traveled old Mr. Toad, hoppity-hop-hop-hop, hoppity-hop-hop-hop, and behind him strolled Tommy. And while old Mr. Toad seemed to be going very fast, and was, for him, Tommy was having hard work to go slow enough to stay behind. And this shows what a difference mere size may make. When they reached the wishing-stone, Mr. Toad was tired from having hurried so, and Tommy was equally tired from the effort of going slow, so both were glad to sit down for a rest. Old Mr. Toad crept in under the edge of the wishing-stone on the shady side, and Tommy, still thinking of old Mr. Toad, sat down on the wishing-stone itself.

"I wonder," he chuckled, "if he has come down here to wish. Perhaps he'll wish himself into something beautiful, as they do in fairy stories. I should think he'd want to. Goodness knows, he's homely enough! It's sad enough to be freckled, but to be covered with warts—ugh! There isn't a single beautiful thing about him."

As he said this, Tommy leaned over that he might better look at old Mr. Toad, and Mr. Toad looked up at Tommy quite as if he understood what Tommy had said, so that Tommy looked straight into Mr. Toad's eyes. It was the first time in all his life that Tommy had ever looked into a toad's eyes. Whoever would think of looking at the eyes of a hop-toad? Certainly not Tommy. Eyes were eyes, and a toad had two of them. Wasn't that enough to know? Why under the sun should a fellow bother about the color of them, or anything like that? What difference did it make? Well, it made just the difference between knowing and not knowing; between knowledge and ignorance; between justice and injustice.

Tommy suddenly realized this as he looked straight into the eyes of old Mr. Toad, and it gave him a funny feeling inside. It was something like that feeling you have when you speak to some one you think is an old friend and find him to be a total stranger. "I—I beg your pardon, Mr. Toad," said he. "I take it all back. You have got something beautiful—the most beautiful eyes I've ever seen. If I had eyes as beautiful as yours, I wouldn't care how many freckles I had. Why haven't I ever seen them before?"

Old Mr. Toad slowly blinked, as much as to say, "That's up to you, young man. They're the same two eyes I've always had. If you haven't learned to use your own eyes, that is no fault and no business of mine. If I made as little use of my eyes as you do of yours, I shouldn't last long."

It never before had occurred to Tommy that there was anything particularly interesting about old Mr. Toad. But those beautiful eyes—for a toad's eyes are

truly beautiful, so beautiful that they are the cause
of the old legend that a toad carries a jewel in his
head—set him to thinking. The more he thought,
the more he realized how very little he knew about
this homely common neighbor of the garden.

"All I know about him is that he eats bugs," muttered Tommy, "and on that account is a pretty good
fellow to have around. My, but he *has* got great eyes!
I wonder if there is anything else interesting about
him. I wonder if I should wish to be a toad just to
learn about him, if I could be one. I guess some of the
wishes I've made on this old stone have been sort of
foolish, because every time I've been discontented
or envious, and I guess the wishes have come true
just to teach me a lesson. I'm not discontented now.
I should say not! A fellow would be pretty poor stuff
to be discontented on a beautiful spring day like
this! And I don't envy old Mr. Toad, not a bit, unless
it's for his beautiful eyes, and I guess that doesn't
count. I don't see how he can have a very interesting life, but I almost want to wish just to see if it *will*
come true."

At that moment, old Mr. Toad came out from
under the wishing-stone and started on down the
Lone Little Path. Just as before, he seemed to be in
a hurry to get somewhere, and to have something
on his mind. Tommy had to smile as he watched his
awkward hops.

"I may as well let him get a good start, because he
goes so awfully slow," thought Tommy, and dreamily

watched until old Mr. Toad was just going out of sight around a turn in the Lone Little Path. Then, instead of getting up and following, Tommy suddenly made up his mind to test the old wishing-stone. "I wish," said he right out aloud, "I wish that I could be a toad!"

No sooner were the words out of his mouth than he was hurrying down the Lone Little Path after old Mr. Toad, hop-hop-hoppity-hop, a toad himself. He knew now just where old Mr. Toad was bound for, and he was in a hurry, a tremendous hurry, to get there himself. It was the Smiling Pool. He didn't know why he wanted to get there, but he did. It seemed to him that he couldn't get there quick enough. It was spring, and the joy of spring made him tingle all over from the tip of his nose to the tips of his toes; but with it was a great longing—a longing for the Smiling Pool. It was a longing very much like homesickness. He felt that he couldn't be really happy until he got there, and that nothing could or should keep him away from there. He couldn't even stop to eat. He knew, too, that that was just the way old Mr. Toad was feeling, and it didn't surprise him as he hurried along, hop-hop-hoppity-hop, to find other toads all headed in the same direction, and all in just as much of a hurry as he was.

Suddenly he heard a sound that made him hurry faster than ever, or at least try to. It was a clear sweet peep, peep, peep. "It's my cousin Stickytoes the Tree-toad, and he's got there before me," thought

Tommy, and tried to hop faster. That single peep grew into a great chorus of peeps, and now he heard other voices, the voices of his other cousins, the frogs. He began to feel that he must sing too, but he couldn't stop for that.

At last, Tommy and old Mr. Toad reached the Smiling Pool, and with a last long hop landed in the shallow water on the edge. How good the cool water felt to his dry skin! At the very first touch, the great longing left Tommy and a great content took its place. He had reached home, and he knew it. It was the same way with old Mr. Toad and with the other toads that kept coming and coming from all directions. And the very first thing that many of them did as soon as they had rested a bit was—what do you think? Why, each one began to sing. Yes, sir, a great many of those toads began to sing! If Tommy had been his true self instead of a toad, he probably would have been more surprised than he was when he discovered that old Mr. Toad had beautiful eyes. But he wasn't surprised now, for the very good reason that he was singing himself.

Tommy could no more help singing than he could help breathing. Just as he had to fill his lungs with air, so he had to give expression to the joy that filled him. He just *had* to. And, as the most natural expression of joy is in song, Tommy added his voice to the great chorus of the Smiling Pool. In his throat was a pouch for which he had not been aware that he had any particular use, but now he found out what it was for. He filled it with air, and it swelled and swelled like a little balloon, until it was actually larger than his head; and, though he wasn't aware of it, he filled it in a very interesting way. He drew the air in through his nostrils and then forced it through two little slits in the floor of his mouth near the forward end of his tongue. All the time he kept his mouth tightly closed. That little balloon was for the purpose of increasing the sound of his voice. Later he discovered that he could sing when wholly under water, with mouth and nostrils tightly closed, by passing the air back and forth between his lungs and that throat-pouch.

It was the same way with all the other toads, and on all sides Tommy saw them sitting upright in the shallow water with their funny swelled-out throats, and singing with all their might. In all the Great World, there was no more joyous place than the Smiling Pool in those beautiful spring days. It seemed as if everybody sang—Redwing the Black-bird in the bulrushes, Little Friend the Song-sparrow in the bushes along the edge of the Laughing Brook, Bubbling Bob the Bobolink in the top of the nearest tree on the Green Meadows, and the toads and frogs in every part of the Smiling Pool. But of all those songs there was none sweeter or more expressive of perfect happiness than that of Tommy and his neighbor, homely, almost ugly-looking, old Mr. Toad.

But it was not quite true that everybody sang. Tommy found it out in a way that put an end to his

Tommy saw them sitting upright in
the shallow water. *Page 98*.

own singing for a little while. Jolly, round, bright Mr. Sun was shining his brightest, and the singers of the Smiling Pool were doing their very best, when suddenly old Mr. Toad cut his song short right in the middle. So did other toads and frogs on both sides of him. Tommy stopped too, just because the others did. There was something fearsome in that sudden ending of glad song. Tommy sat perfectly still with a queer feeling that something dreadful was happening. He didn't move, but he rolled his eyes this way and that way until he saw something moving on the edge of the shore. It was Mr. Blacksnake, just starting to crawl away, and from his mouth two long legs were feebly kicking. One of the sweet singers would sing no more. After that, no matter how glad and happy he felt as he sang, he kept a sharp watch all the time for Mr. Snake, for he had learned that there was danger even in the midst of joy.

But when the dusk of evening came, he knew that Mr. Snake was no longer to be feared, and he sang in perfect peace and contentment until there came an evening when again that mighty chorus stopped abruptly. A shadow passed over him. Looking up, he saw a great bird with soundless wings, and hanging from its claws one of the sweet singers whose voice was stilled forever. Hooty the Owl had caught his supper. So Tommy learned that not all animal-folk sing their joy in spring, and that those who do not, such as Mr. Blacksnake and Hooty the Owl, were to be watched out for.

"Too bad, too bad!" whispered old Mr. Toad as they waited for some one to start the chorus again. "That fellow was careless. He didn't watch out. He forgot. Bad business, forgetting; bad business. Doesn't do at all. Now I've lived a great many years, and I expect to live a great many more. I never forget to watch out. We toads haven't very many enemies, and if we watch out for the few we have got, there isn't much to worry about. It's safe to start that chorus again, so here goes."

He swelled his throat out and began to sing. In five minutes it was as if nothing had happened at the Smiling Pool.

So the glad spring passed, and Tommy saw many things of interest. He saw thousands of tiny eggs hatch into funny little tadpoles, and for a while it was hard to tell at first glance the toad tadpoles from their cousins, the frog tadpoles. But the little toad babies grew fast, and it was almost no time at all before they were not tadpoles at all, but tiny little toads with tails. Day by day the tails grew shorter, until there were no tails at all, each baby a perfect little toad no bigger than a good-sized cricket, but big enough to consider that he had outgrown his nursery, and to be eager to leave the Smiling Pool and go out into the Great World.

"Foolish! Foolish! Much better off here. Got a lot to learn before they can take care of themselves in the Great World," grumbled old Mr. Toad. Then he chuckled. "Know just how they feel, though," said he. "Felt the same way myself at their age. Suppose you did, too."

Of course, Tommy, never having been little like that, for he had wished himself into a full-grown toad, had no such memory. But old Mr. Toad didn't seem to expect a reply, for he went right on: "Took care of myself, and I guess those little rascals can do the same thing. By the way, this water is getting uncomfortably warm. Besides, I've got business to attend to. Can't sing all the time. Holidays are over. Think I'll start along back to-night. Are you going my way?"

Now Tommy hadn't thought anything about the matter. He had noticed that a great many toads were leaving the Smiling Pool, and that he himself didn't care so much about singing. Then, too, he longed for a good meal, for he had eaten little since coming to the Smiling Pool. So when old Mr. Toad asked if he was going his way, Tommy suddenly decided that he was.

"Good!" replied old Mr. Toad. "We'll start as soon as it begins to grow dark. It's safer then. Besides, I never could travel in bright, hot weather. It's bad for the health."

So when the black shadows began to creep across the Green Meadows, old Mr. Toad and Tommy turned their backs on the Smiling Pool and started up the Lone Little Path. They were not in a hurry now, as they had been when they came down the Lone Little Path, and they hopped along slowly, stopping to hunt bugs and slugs and worms, for they were very, very hungry. Old Mr. Toad fixed his eyes on a fly which had just lighted on the ground two inches in front of him. He sat perfectly still, but there was a lightning-like flash of something pink from his mouth, and the fly was gone. Mr. Toad smacked his lips.

"I don't see how some people get along with their tongues fastened 'way back in their throats," he remarked. "The proper place for a tongue to be fastened is the way ours are—by the front end. Then you can shoot it out its whole length and get your meal every time. See that spider over there? If I tried to get any nearer, he'd be gone at the first move. He's a goner anyway. Watch!" There was that little pink flash again, and, sure enough, the spider had disappeared. Once more old Mr. Toad smacked his lips. "Didn't I tell you he was a goner?" said he, chuckling over his own joke.

Tommy quite agreed with old Mr. Toad. That arrangement of his tongue certainly was most convenient. Any insect he liked to eat that came within two inches of his nose was as good as caught. All he had to do was to shoot out his tongue, which was sticky, and when he drew it back, it brought the bug with it and carried it well down his throat to a comfortable point to swallow. Yes, it certainly was convenient.

It took so much time to fill their stomachs that they did not travel far that night. The next day they spent under an old barrel, where they buried

Once more old Mr. Toad smacked his lips. *Page 103.*

themselves in the soft earth by digging holes with their stout hind feet and backing in at the same time until just their noses and eyes showed at the door-ways, ready to snap up any foolish bugs or worms who might seek shelter in their hiding-place. It was such a comfortable place that they stayed several days, going out nights to hunt, and returning at daylight.

It was while they were there that old Mr. Toad complained that his skin was getting too tight and uncomfortable, and announced that he was going to change it. And he did. It was a pretty tiresome pro-cess, and required a lot of wriggling and kicking, but little by little the old skin split in places and Mr. Toad worked it off, getting his hind legs free first, and later his hands, using the latter to pull the last of it from the top of his head over his eyes. And, as fast as he worked it loose, he swallowed it!

"Now I feel better," said he, as with a final gulp he swallowed the last of his old suit. Tommy wasn't sure that he *looked* any better, for the new skin looked very much like the old one; but he didn't say so.

Tommy found that he needed four good meals a day, and filling his stomach took most of his time when he wasn't resting. Cutworms he found es-pecially to his liking, and it was astonishing how many he could eat in a night. Caterpillars of many kinds helped out, and it was great fun to sit beside an ant-hill and snap up the busy workers as they came out.

But, besides their daily foraging, there was plenty of excitement, as when a rustling warned them that a snake was near, or a shadow on the grass told them that a hawk was sailing overhead. At those times they simply sat perfectly still, and looked so much like little lumps of earth that they were not seen at all, or, if they were, they were not recognized. Instead of drinking, they soaked water in through the skin. To have a dry skin was to be terribly uncomfortable, and that is why they always sought shelter during the sunny hours.

At last came a rainy day. "Toad weather! Perfect toad weather!" exclaimed old Mr. Toad. "This is the day to travel."

So once more they took up their journey in a leisurely way. A little past noon, the clouds cleared away and the sun came out bright. "Time to get under cover," grunted old Mr. Toad, and led the way to a great gray rock beside the Lone Little Path and crawled under the edge of it. Tommy was just going to follow—when something happened! He wasn't a toad at all—just a freckle-faced boy sitting on the wishing-stone. He pinched himself to make sure. Then he looked under the edge of the wishing-stone for old Mr. Toad. He wasn't there. Gradually he remembered that he had seen old Mr. Toad disappearing around a turn in the Lone Little Path, going hoppity-hop-hop-hop, as if he had something on his mind.

"Toad weather! Perfect toad weather!"
exclaimed old Mr. Toad. *Page 106.*

"And I thought that there was nothing interesting about a toad!" muttered Tommy. "I wonder if it's all true. I believe I'll run down to the Smiling Pool and just see if that is where Mr. Toad really was going. He must have about reached there by this time."

He jumped to his feet and ran down the Lone Little Path. As he drew near the Smiling Pool, he stopped to listen to the joyous chorus rising from it. He had always thought of the singers as just "peepers," or frogs. Now, for the first time, he noticed that there were different voices. Just ahead of him he saw something moving. It was old Mr. Toad. Softly, very softly, Tommy followed and saw him jump into the shallow water. Carefully he tiptoed nearer and watched. Presently old Mr. Toad's throat began to swell and swell, until it was bigger than his head. Then he began to sing. It was only a couple of notes, tremulous and wonderfully sweet, and so expressive of joy and gladness that Tommy felt his own heart swell with happiness.

"It is true!" he cried. "And all the rest must be true. And I said there was nothing beautiful about a toad, when all the time he has the most wonderful eyes and the sweetest voice I've ever heard. It must be true about that queer tongue, and the way he sheds his skin. I'm going to watch and see for myself. Why, I've known old Mr. Toad all my life, and thought him just a common fellow, when all the time he is just wonderful! I'm glad I've been a toad. Of course there is nothing like being a boy, but I'd rather be a toad than some other things I've been on the old wishing-stone. I'm going to get all the toads I can to live in my garden this summer."

And that is just what Tommy did do, with the result that he had one of the best gardens anywhere around. And nobody knew why but Tommy—and his friends, the toads.

VII
Why Tommy Took Up All His Traps

IF there was one thing that Tommy enjoyed above another, it was trapping. There were several reasons why he enjoyed it. In the first place, it took him out of doors with something definite to do. He loved the meadows and the woods and the pastures, and all the beauties of them with which Old Mother Nature is so lavish. He loved to tramp along the Laughing Brook and around the Smiling Pool. Always, no matter what the time of year, there was something interesting to see. Now it was a flower new to him, or a bird that he had not seen before. Again it was a fleeting glimpse of one of the shy, fleet-footed little people who wear coats of fur. He liked these best of all because they were the hardest to surprise and study at their home life. And that was one reason why he enjoyed trapping so much. It was matching his wits against their wits. And one other reason was the money which he got for the pelts.

So Tommy was glad when the late fall came and it was time to set traps and every morning make his rounds to see what he had caught. In the coldest part of the winter, when the snow was deep and the ice was thick, he stopped trapping, but he began again with the beginning of spring when the Laughing

Brook was once more set free and the Smiling Pool no longer locked in icy fetters. It was then that the muskrats and the minks became most active, and their fur coats were still at their best. You see the more active they were, the more likely they were to step into one of his traps.

On this particular afternoon, after school, Tommy had come down to the Smiling Pool to set a few extra traps for muskrats. The trapping season, that is the season when the fur was still at its best, or "prime," as the fur dealers call it, would soon be at an end. He had set a trap on an old log which lay partly in and partly out of the water. He knew that the muskrats used this old log to sun themselves because one had plunged off it as he came up. So he set a trap just under water on the end of the old log where the first muskrat who tried to climb out there would step in it.

"I'll get one here, as sure as shooting," said Tommy.

Then he found a little grassy tussock, and he knew by the matted-down grass that it was a favorite resting place for muskrats. Here he set another trap and left some slices of carrot as bait. By the merest accident, he found a hole in the bank and, from the look of it, he felt sure that it had been made by one of the furry little animals he wanted to catch. Right at the very entrance he set another trap, and artfully covered it with water-soaked leaves from the bottom of the Smiling Pool so that it could not be seen.

"I'd like to see anything go in or out of that hole without getting caught," said he, with an air of being mightily tickled with himself and his own smartness.

So he went on until he had set all his traps, and all the time he was very happy. Spring had come, and it is everybody's right to be happy in the spring. He heard the joyous notes of the first birds who had come on the lagging heels of winter from the warm southland, and they made him want to sing, himself. Everything about him proclaimed new life and the joy of living. He could feel it in the very air. It was good to be alive.

After the last trap had been put in place, he sat down on an old log to rest for a few minutes and enjoy the scene. The Smiling Pool was as smooth as polished glass. Presently, as Tommy sat there without moving, two little silver lines, which met and formed a V, started on the farther side of the Smiling Pool and came straight toward him. Tommy knew what those silver lines were. They were the wake made by a swimming muskrat.

"My! I wish I'd brought my gun!" thought Tommy. "It's queer how a fellow always sees things when he hasn't got a gun, and never sees them when he has."

He could perceive the little brown head very plainly now, and, as it drew nearer, he could distinguish the outline of the body just under the surface, and back of that the queer, rubbery, flattened tail set edge-wise in the water and moving rapidly from side to side.

"It's a regular propeller," thought Tommy, "and he certainly knows how to use it. It sculls him right along. If he should lose that, he sure would be up against it!"

Tommy moved ever so little, so as to get a better view. Instantly there was a sharp slap of the tail on the water, a plunge, and only a ripple to show that a second before there had been a swimmer there. Two other slaps and plunges sounded from distant parts of the Smiling Pool and Tommy knew that he would see no more muskrats unless he sat very still for a long time. Slowly he got to his feet, stretched, and then started for home. All the way across the Green Meadows he kept thinking of that little glimpse of muskrat life he had had, and for the first time in his life he began to think that there might be something more interesting about a muskrat than his fur coat. Always before, he had thought of a muskrat as simply a rat, a big, overgrown cousin of the pests that stole the grain in the hen-house, and against whom every man's hand is turned, as it should be.

But somehow that little glimpse of Jerry Muskrat at home had awakened a new interest. It struck him quite suddenly that it was a very wonderful thing that an animal breathing air, just as he did himself, could be so at home in the water and disappear so suddenly and completely.

"It's a regular propeller," thought Tommy. *Page 113*.

"It must be great to be able to swim like that!" thought Tommy as he sat down on the wishing-stone, and looked back across the Green Meadows to the Smiling Pool. "I wonder what he does down there under water. Now I think of it, I don't know much about him except that he is the only rat with a fur that is good for anything. If it wasn't for that fur coat of his, I don't suppose anybody would bother him. What a snap he would have then! I'll bet he has no end of fun in the summer, with nothing to worry about and plenty to eat, and always cool and comfortable no matter what the weather! What gets me is how he spends the winter when everything is frozen. He must be under the ice for weeks. I wonder if he sleeps the way the woodchuck does. I suppose I can find out just by wishing, seeing that I'm sitting right here on the old wishing-stone. It would be a funny thing to do to wish myself into a rat. It doesn't seem as if there could be anything very interesting about the life of anything so stupid-looking as a muskrat, and yet I've thought the same thing about some other critters and found I was wrong."

He gazed dreamily down toward the Smiling Pool, and, the longer he looked, the more he wondered what it would be like to live there. At last, almost without knowing it, he said the magic words.

"I—I wish I were a muskrat!" he murmured.

Tommy was in the Smiling Pool. He was little and fur-coated, with a funny little flattened tail. And he really had two coats, the outer of long hairs, a sort of water-proof, while the under coat was soft and fine and meant to keep him warm. And, though he was swimming with only his head out of water, he wasn't wet at all.

It was a beautiful summer evening, just at the hour of twilight, and the Smiling Pool was very beautiful, the most beautiful place that ever was. At least it seemed so to Tommy. In the bulrushes a few little feathered folks were still twittering sleepily. Over on his big green lily-pad Grandfather Frog was leading the frog chorus in a great deep voice. From various places in the Smiling Pool came sharp little squeaks and faint splashes. It was playtime for little musk-rats and visiting time for big muskrats. An odor of musk filled the air and was very pleasant to Tommy as he sniffed and sniffed. He was playing hide-and-seek and tag with other little muskrats of his own age, and not one of them had a care in all the world. Far away, Hooty the Owl was sending forth his fierce hunting call, but no one in the Smiling Pool took the least notice of it. By and by it ceased.

Tommy was chasing one of his playmates in and out among the bulrushes. Twice they had been warned by a wise old muskrat not to go beyond the line of bulrushes into the open water. But little folks are forgetful, especially when playing. Tommy's little playmate forgot. In the excitement of getting away from Tommy he swam out where the first little star was reflected in the Smiling Pool. A shadow passed over Tommy, and hardly had it passed when there

It was playtime for the little muskrats. *Page 116.*

was a sharp slap of something striking the water. Tommy knew what it was. He knew that it was the tail of some watchful old muskrat who had discovered danger, and that it meant "dive at once." Tommy dived. He didn't wait to learn what the danger was, but promptly filled his little lungs with air, plunged under water and swam as far as he could. When he just had to come up for more air, he put only his nose out and this in the darkest place he knew of among the rushes.

There he remained perfectly still. Down inside, his heart was thumping with fear of he knew not what. There wasn't a sound to be heard around the Smiling Pool. It was as still as if there were no living thing there. After what seemed like a long, long time, the deep voice of Grandfather Frog boomed out, and then the squeak of the old muskrat who had given the alarm told all within hearing that all was safe again. At once, all fear left Tommy and he swam to find his playmates.

"What was it?" he asked one of them.

"Hooty, the Owl," was the reply. "Didn't you see him?"

"I saw a shadow," replied Tommy.

"That was Hooty. I wonder if he caught anybody," returned the other.

Tommy didn't say anything, but he thought of the playmate who forgot and swam out beyond the bulrushes, and, when he had hunted and hunted and couldn't find him, he knew that Hooty had not visited the Smiling Pool for nothing.

So Tommy learned the great lesson of never being careless and forgetting. Later that same night, as he sat on a little muddy platform on the edge of the water eating a delicious tender young lily-root, there came that same warning slap of a tail on the water. Tommy didn't wait for even one more nibble, but plunged into the deepest water and hid as before. This time when the signal that all was well was given he learned that some one with sharper ears than his had heard the footsteps of a fox on the shore and had given the warning just in the nick of time. Four things Tommy learned that night. First, that, safe and beautiful as it seems, the Smiling Pool is not free from dangers for little muskrats; second, that forget-fulness means a short life; third, that to dive at the instant a danger-signal is sounded and inquire later what the danger was is the only sure way of being safe; and fourth, that it is the duty of every muskrat who detects danger to warn every other muskrat.

Though he didn't realize it then, this last was the most important lesson of all. It was the great lesson that human beings have been so long learning, and which many have not learned yet, that, just in pro-portion as each one looks out for the welfare of his neighbors, he is himself better off. Instead of having just one pair of little eyes and one pair of keen little ears to guard him against danger Tommy had many pairs of little eyes and little ears keeping guard all the time, some of them better than his own.

Eating, sleeping, and playing, and of course watching out for danger, were all that Tommy had to think about through the long lazy summer, and he grew and grew and grew until he was as big as the biggest muskrats in the Smiling Pool, and could come and go as he pleased. There was less to fear now from Hooty the Owl, for Hooty prefers tender young muskrats. He had learned all about the ways of Reddy Fox, and feared him not at all. He had learned where the best lily-roots grow, and how to find and open mussels, those clams which live in fresh water. He had a favorite old log, half in the water, to which he brought these to open them and eat them, and more than one fight did he have before his neighbors learned to respect this as his. He had explored all the shore of the Smiling Pool and knew every hole in the banks. He had even been some distance up the Laughing Brook. Life was very joyous.

But, as summer began to wane, the days to grow shorter and the nights longer, he discovered that playtime was over. At least, all his friends and neighbors seemed to think so, for they were very, very busy. Something inside told him that it was time, high time, that he also went to work. Cold weather was coming and he must be prepared. For one thing he must have a comfortable home, and the only way to get one was to make one for himself. Of course this meant work, but somehow Tommy felt that he would feel happier if he did work. He was tired of doing nothing in particular. In his roamings about, he had seen many muskrat homes, some of them old and deserted, and some of them visited while the owners were away. He knew just what a first-class house should be like. It should be high enough in the bank to be above water at all times, even during the spring floods, and it should be reached by a passage the entrance to which should at all times be under water, even in the driest season.

On the bank of the Smiling Pool grew a tree, and the spreading roots came down so that some of them were in the Smiling Pool itself. Under them, Tommy made the entrance to his burrow. The roots hid it. At first the digging was easy, for the earth was little more than mud; but, as the passage slanted up, the digging became harder. Still he kept at it. Two or three times he stopped and decided that he had gone far enough, then changed his mind and kept on. At last he found a place to suit him, and there he made a snug chamber not very far under the grass-roots.

When he had finished it, he was very proud of it. He told Jerry Muskrat about it. "Have you more than one entrance to it?" asked Jerry.

"No," replied Tommy, "it was hard enough work to make that one."

Jerry turned up his nose. "That wouldn't do for me," he declared. "A house with only one entrance is nothing but a trap. Supposing a fierce old mink

"Have you more than one entrance to
it?" asked Jerry. *Page 121*.

should find that doorway while you were inside; what would you do then?"

Tommy hadn't thought of that. Once more he went to work, and made another long tunnel leading up to that snug chamber; and then, perhaps because he had got the habit, he made a third. From one of these tunnels he even made a short branch with a carefully hidden opening right out on the meadow, for Tommy liked to prowl around on land once in a while. The chamber he lined with grass and old rushes until he had a very comfortable bed.

With all this hard work completed, you would have supposed that Tommy would have been satisfied, wouldn't you? But he wasn't. He found that some of his neighbors were building houses of a wholly different kind, and right away he decided that he must have one too. So he chose a place where the water was shallow, and not too far from the place where the water-lilies grew; and there among the bulrushes he once more set to work. This time he dug out the mud and the roots of the rushes, piling them around him until he was in a sort of little well. From this he dug several tunnels leading to the deep water where he could be sure that the entrance never would be frozen over. The mud and sods he piled up until they came above the water, and then he made a platform of rushes and mud with an opening in the middle down into that well from which his tunnels radiated. On this platform he built a great mound of rushes, and grass, and even twigs, all wattled together. Some of them he had to bring clear from the other side of the Smiling Pool. And, as he built that mound, he made a nice large room in the middle, biting off all the ends of sticks and rushes which happened to be in the way. When he had made that room to suit him, he made a comfortable bed there, just as he had in the house in the bank. Then he built the walls very thick, adding rushes and mud and sods all around except on the very top. There he left the roof thinner, with little spaces for the air to get in, for of course he must have air to breathe.

When at last the new house was finished, he was very proud of it. There were two rooms, the upper one with its comfortable bed quite above the water, and the lower one wholly under water, connected with the former by a little doorway. The only way of getting into the house was by one of his tunnels to the lower room. When all was done, an old muskrat looked it over and told him that he had done very well for a young fellow, which made Tommy feel very important.

The weather was growing cool now, so Tommy laid up some supplies in both houses and then spent his spare time calling on his neighbors. By this time he had grown a fine thick coat and didn't mind at all how cold it grew. In fact he liked the cold weather. It was about this time that he had a dreadful experience. He climbed out one evening on his favorite log to open and eat a mussel he had found.

Tommy went calling on his neighbors. *Page 124.*

There was a snap, and something caught him by the tail and pinched dreadfully. He pulled with all his might, but the dreadful thing wouldn't let go. He turned and bit at it, but it was harder than his teeth and gnaw as he would he could make no impression on it. A great terror filled his heart and he struggled and pulled, heedless of the pain, until he was too tired to struggle longer. He just had to lie still. After a while, when he had regained his strength, he struggled again. This time he felt his tail give a little. A neighbor swam over to see what all the fuss was about. "It's a trap," said he. "It's lucky you are not caught by a foot instead of by the tail. If you keep on pulling you may get free. I did once."

This gave Tommy new hope and he struggled harder than ever. At last he fell headlong into the water. The cruel steel jaws had not been able to keep his tapered tail from slipping between them. He was free, but oh, so frightened!

After that Tommy grew wise. He never went ashore without first examining the place for one of those dreadful traps, and he found more than one. It got so that he gave up all his favorite places and made new ones. Once he found one of his friends caught by a forefoot and he was actually cutting his foot off with his sharp teeth. It was dreadful, but it was the only way of saving his life.

Those were sad and terrible times around the Smiling Pool and along the Laughing Brook for the people in fur, but there didn't seem to be anything they could do about it except to everlastingly watch out. One morning Tommy awoke to find the Smiling Pool covered with ice. He liked it. A sense of great peace fell on the Smiling Pool. There was no more danger from traps except around certain spring holes, and there was no need of going there. Much of the time Tommy slept in that fine house of rushes and mud. Its walls had frozen solid and it was as comfortable as could be imagined. A couple of friends who had no house stayed with him. When they were hungry all they had to do was to drop down into the tunnel leading to deep water and so out into the Smiling Pool under the ice, dig up a lily-root and swim back and eat it in comfort inside the house. If they got short of air while swimming under the ice they were almost sure to find little air spaces under the edge of the banks. No matter how bitter the cold or how wild the storm above the ice,—below it was always calm and the temperature never changed.

Sometimes Tommy went over to his house in the bank. Once, while he was there, a blood-thirsty mink followed him. Tommy heard him coming and escaped down one of the other passages. Then he was thankful indeed that he had made more than one. But this was his only adventure all the long winter. At last spring came, the ice disappeared and the water rose in the Laughing Brook until it was above the banks, and in the Smiling Pool until Tommy's house was nearly under water. Then he moved over to his house in the bank and was comfortable again.

One day he swam over to his house of rushes and climbed up on the top. He had no thought of danger there and he was heedless. Snap! A trap set right on top of the house held him fast by one leg. A mist swam before his eyes as he looked across the Green Meadows and heard the joyous carol of Welcome Robin. Why, oh why, should there be such misery in the midst of so much joy? He was trying to make up his mind to lose his foot when, far up on the edge of the meadows, he saw an old gray rock. Somehow the sight of it brought a vague sense of comfort to him. He strained his eyes to see it better and— Tommy was just himself, rubbing his eyes as he sat on the old wishing-stone.

"—I was just going to cut my foot off. Ugh!" he shuddered. "Two or three times I've found a foot in my traps, but I never realized before what it really meant. Why, those little chaps had more nerve than I'll ever have!"

He gazed thoughtfully down toward the Smiling Pool. Then suddenly he sprang to his feet and began to run toward it. "It's too late to take all of 'em up to-night," he muttered, "but I'll take what I can, and to-morrow morning I'll take up the rest. I hope nothing will get caught in 'em. I never knew before how dreadful it must be to be caught in a trap. I'll never set another trap as long as I live, so there! Why, Jerry Muskrat is almost as wonderful as Paddy the Beaver, and he doesn't do anything a bit of harm. I didn't know he was so interesting.

He hasn't as many troubles as some, but he has enough, I guess, without me adding to them. Say, that's a great life he leads! If it wasn't for traps, it wouldn't be half bad to be a muskrat. Of course it's better to be a boy, but I can tell you right now I'm going to be a better boy—less thoughtless and cruel. Jerry Muskrat, you haven't anything more to fear from me, not a thing! I take off my hat to you for a busy little worker, and for having more nerve than any *boy* I know."

And never again did Tommy set a trap for little wild folk.

VIII

How Tommy Learned to Admire
Thunderer the Ruffed Grouse

FROM over in the Green Forest where the silver
beeches grow, came a sound which made Tommy
stop to listen. For a minute or two all was still. Then
it came again, a deep, throbbing sound that began
slowly and then grew faster and faster until it ended
in a long rumble like distant thunder. Tommy knew
it couldn't be that, for there wasn't a cloud in the
sky; and anyway it wasn't the season of thunder-
storms. Again he heard that deep hollow throbbing
grow fast and faster until there was no time between
the beats and it became a thunderous rumble; and
for some reason which he could not have explained,
Tommy felt his pulse beat faster in unison, and a
strange sense of joyous exhilaration.

*Drum—drum—drum—drum—drum, drum, drum,
dr-r-r-r-r-um!* The sound beat out from beyond the
hemlocks and rolled away through the woods.

"It's an old cock-partridge drummin'." Tommy
had a way of talking to himself when he was alone.
"He's down on that old beech log at the head of the
gully. Gee, I'd like to see him! Bet it's the same one
that was there last year. Dad says that old log is a
reg'lar drummin'-log and he's seen partridges drum

there lots of times. And yet he doesn't really know how they make all that noise. Says some folks say they beat the log with their wings, and, because it's holler, it makes that sound. Don't believe it, though. They'd bu'st their wings doing that. Besides, that old log ain't much holler anyway, and I never can make it sound up much hammering it with a stick; so how could a partridge do it with nothin' but his wings?

"Some other folks say they do it by hitting their wings together over their backs; but I don't see any sense in that, 'cause their wings are all feathers. And some say they beat their sides to make the noise; but if they do that, I should think they'd knock all the wind out of themselves and be too sore to move. Bet if I could ever catch ol' Thunderer drummin', I'd find out how he does it! I know what I'll do! I'll go over to the old wishing-stone. Wonder why I didn't think of it before. Bet I'll find out a lot."

He thrust his hands into his pockets and trudged up the Crooked Little Path, out of the Green Forest, and over to the great gray stone on the edge of the Green Meadows where so many wishes had come true, or had seemed to come true, anyway, and where he had learned so much about the lives of his little wild neighbors. As he tramped, his thoughts were all of Thunderer the Ruffed Grouse, whom he called a partridge, and some other people call a pheasant, but who is neither. Many times had Tommy been startled by having the handsome bird spring into the air from almost under his feet, with a noise of wings that was enough to scare any-body. It was because of this and the noise of his drumming that Tommy called him Thunderer.

With a long sigh of satisfaction, for he was tired, Tommy sat down on the wishing-stone, planted his elbows on his knees, dropped his chin in his hands, looked over to the Green Forest through half-closed eyes, and wished.

"I wish," said he, slowly and earnestly, "I could be a partridge." He meant, of course, that he could be a grouse.

Just as always had happened when he had ex-pressed such a wish on the old wishing-stone, the very instant the words were out of his mouth, he ceased to be a boy. He was a tiny little bird, like noth-ing so much as a teeny, weeny chicken, a soft little ball of brown and yellow, one of a dozen, who all looked alike as they scurried after their little brown mother in answer to her anxious cluck. Behind them, on the ground, cunningly hidden back of a fallen tree, was an empty nest with only some bits of shell as a reminder that, just a few hours before, it had contained twelve buff eggs. Now Tommy and his brothers and sisters didn't give the old nest so much as a thought. They had left it as soon as they were strong enough to run. They were starting out for their first lesson in the school of the Great World.

Perhaps Tommy thought his mother fussy and altogether a great deal too nervous; but if he did, he didn't say so. There was one thing that seemed to have been born in him, something that as a boy he had to learn, and that was the habit of instant obedience. It was instinct, which, so naturalists say, is habit confirmed and handed down through many generations. Tommy didn't know why he obeyed. He just did, that was all. It didn't occur to him that there was anything else to do. The idea of disobeying never entered his funny, pretty little head. And it was just so with all the others. Mother Grouse had only to speak and they did just exactly what she told them to.

This habit of obedience on their part took a great load from the mind of Mother Grouse. They hadn't been in the Great World long enough to know, but she knew that there were dangers on every side; and to watch out for and protect them from these she needed all her senses, and she couldn't afford to dull any of them by useless worrying. So it was a great relief to her to know that, when she had bidden them hide and keep perfectly still until she called them, they would do exactly as she said. This made it possible for her to leave them long enough to lead an enemy astray, and be sure that when she returned she would find them just where she had left them.

She had to do this twice on their very first journey into the Great World. Tommy was hurrying along with the others as fast as his small legs could take him when his mother gave a sharp but low call to hide. There was a dried leaf on the ground close to Tommy. Instantly he crept under it and flattened

Mother Grouse knew there were dangers
on every side.   *Page 133.*

his small self to the ground, closed his eyes tight, and listened with all his might. He heard the whirr of strong wings as Mother Grouse took flight. If he had peeped out, he would have seen that she flew only a very little way, and that, when she came to earth again, there appeared to be something the matter with her, so that she flopped along instead of running or flying. But he didn't see this, because he was under that dead leaf and his eyes were tightly closed.

Presently, the ground vibrated under the steps of heavy feet that all but trod on the leaf under which Tommy lay and frightened him terribly. But he did not move and he made no sound. Again, had he peeped out, he would have seen Mother Grouse fluttering along the ground just ahead of an eager boy who thought to catch her and tried and tried until he had been led far from the place where her babies were. Then all was still, so still that surely there could be no danger near. Surely it was safe to come out now. But Tommy didn't move, nor did any of his brothers and sisters. They had been told not to until they were called, and it never once entered their little heads to disobey. Mother knew best.

At last there came a gentle cluck. Instantly Tommy popped out from under his leaf to see his brothers and sisters popping out from the most unexpected places all about him. It seemed almost as if they had popped out of the very ground itself. And there was Mother Grouse, very proud and very fussy, as she made sure that all her babies were there. Later that same day the same thing happened, only this time there was no heavy footstep, but the lightest kind of patter as cushioned feet eagerly hurried past, and Reddy Fox sprang forward, sure that Mother Grouse was to make him the dinner he liked best, and thus was led away to a safe distance, there to realize how completely he had been fooled.

It was a wonderful day, that first day. There was a great ant-hill which Mother Grouse scratched open with her stout claws and exposed ever and ever so many white things, which were the eggs of the big black ants, and which were delicious eating, as Tommy soon found out. It was great fun to scramble for them, and eat and eat until not another one could be swallowed. And when the shadows began to creep through the Green Forest, they nestled close under Mother Grouse in one of her favorite secret hiding-places and straightway went to sleep as healthy children should, sure that no harm could befall them, nor once guessed how lightly their mother slept and more than once shivered with fear, not for herself but for them, as some prowler of the night passed their retreat.

So the days passed and Tommy grew and learned, and it was a question which he did the faster. The down with which he had been covered gave way to real feathers and he grew real wings, so that he was little over a week old when he could fly in case of need. And in that same length of time, short as it was, he had filled his little head with knowledge. He had learned that a big sandy dome in a sunny spot in the woods usually meant an ants' castle, where he could eat to his heart's content if only it was torn open for him. He had learned that luscious fat worms and bugs were to be found under rotting pieces of bark and the litter of decaying old logs and stumps. He had learned that wild strawberries and some other berries afforded a welcome variety to his bill of fare. He had learned that a daily bath in fine dust was necessary for cleanliness as well as being vastly comforting. He had learned that danger lurked in the air as well as on the ground, for a swooping hawk had caught one of his brothers who had not instantly heeded his mother's warning. But most important of all, he had learned the value of that first lesson in obedience, and to trust wholly to the wisdom of Mother Grouse and never to question her commands.

A big handsome grouse had joined them now. It was old Thunderer, and sometimes when he would throw back his head, spread his beautiful tail until it was like a fan, raise the crest on his head and the glossy ruff on his neck, and proudly strut ahead of them, Tommy thought him the most beautiful sight in all the world and wondered if ever he would grow to be half as handsome. While he did little work in the care of the brood, Thunderer was of real help to Mother Grouse in guarding the little family from ever-lurking dangers. There was no eye or ear more keen

Bugs were to be found under old logs. *Page 137*.

than his, and none more skilful than he in confusing and baffling a hungry enemy who had chanced to discover the presence of the little family. Tommy watched him every minute he could spare from the ever important business of filling his crop, and stored up for future need the things he learned.

Once he ventured to ask Thunderer what was the greatest danger for which a grouse must watch out, and he never forgot the answer.

"There is no greatest danger while you are young," replied Thunderer, shaking out his feathers. "Every danger is greatest while it exists. Never forget that. Never treat any danger lightly. Skunks and foxes and weasels and minks and coons and hawks and owls are equally dangerous to youngsters like you, and one is as much to be feared as another. It is only when you have become full-grown, like me, and then only in the fall of the year, that you will know the greatest danger."

"And what is that?" asked Tommy timidly.

"A man with a gun," replied Thunderer.

"And what is that?" asked Tommy again, eager for knowledge.

"A great creature who walks on two legs and points a stick which spits fire and smoke, and makes a great noise, and kills while it is yet a long distance off."

"Oh!" gasped Tommy. "How is one ever to learn to avoid such a dreadful danger as that?"

"I'll teach you when the time comes," replied Thunderer. "Now run along and take your dust-bath.

You must first learn to avoid other dangers before you will be fitted to meet the greatest danger."

All that long bright summer Tommy thought of that greatest danger, and, by learning how to meet other dangers, tried to prepare himself for it. Sometimes he wondered if there really could be any greater danger than those about him every day. It seemed sometimes as if all the world sought to kill him, who was so harmless himself. Not only were there dangers from hungry animals, and robbers of the air, but also from the very creatures that furnished him much of his living—the tribe of insects. An ugly-looking insect, called a tick, with wicked blood-sucking jaws, killed one of the brood while they were yet small, and an equally ugly worm called a bot-worm caused the death of another. Shadow the Weasel surprised one foolish bird who insisted on sleeping on the ground when he was big enough to know better, and Reddy Fox dined on another whose curiosity led him to move when he had been warned to lie perfectly still, and who paid for his disobedience with his life. Tommy, not three feet away, saw it all and profited by the lesson.

He was big enough now to act for himself and no longer depended wholly for safety on the wisdom of Mother Grouse and Thunderer. But while he trusted to his own senses and judgment, he was ever heedful of their example and still ready to learn. Especially did he take pains to keep near Thunderer and study him and his ways, for he was wise and

Reddy Fox dined on one. *Page 140.*

cunning with the cunning of experience and knowledge. Tommy was filled with great admiration for him and tried to copy him in everything. Thus it was that he learned that there were two ways of flying, one without noise and the other with the thunder of whirring wings. Also he learned that there was a time for each. When he knew himself to be alone and suddenly detected the approach of an enemy, he often would launch himself into the air on silent wings before his presence had been discovered. But when others of his family were near, he would burst into the air with all the noise he could make as a warning to others. Also, it sometimes startled and confused the enemy.

Thunderer had taught him the trick one day when a fox had stolen, unseen by Tommy, almost within jumping distance. Thunderer had seen him, and purposely had waited until the fox was just gathering himself to spring on the unsuspecting Tommy. Then with a splendid roar of his stout wings Thunderer had risen just to one side of the fox, so startling him and distracting his attention that Tommy had had ample time to whirr up in his turn, to the discomfiture of Reynard.

So, when the fall came, Tommy was big from good living, and filled with the knowledge that makes for long life among grouse. He knew the best scratching-grounds, the choicest feeding-places according to the month, every bramble-tangle and every brush-pile, the place for the warmest sun-bath, and the trees which afforded the safest and most comfortable roosting places at night. He knew the ways and the favorite hunting-grounds of every fox, and weasel, and skunk, and coon of the neighborhood, and how to avoid them. He knew when it was safest to lie low and trust to the protective coloring of his feathers, and when it was best to roar away on thundering wings.

The days grew crisp and shorter. The maples turned red and yellow, and soon the woods were filled with fluttering leaves and the trees began to grow bare. It was then that old Thunderer warned Tommy that the season of greatest danger was at hand. Somehow, in the confidence of his strength and the joy of the splendid tide of life surging through him, he didn't fear this unknown danger as he had when as a little fellow he had first heard of it. Then one day, quite unexpectedly, he faced it.

He and Thunderer had been resting quietly in a bramble-tangle on the very edge of the Green Forest, when suddenly there was the rustle of padded feet among the leaves just outside the brambles. Looking out, Tommy saw what at first he took to be a strange and very large kind of fox, and he prepared to fly.

"Not yet! Not yet!" warned Thunderer. "That is a dog and he will not harm us. But to fly now might be to go straight into that greatest danger, of which I had told you. That is the mistake young grouse often make, flying before they know just where the danger is. Watch until you see the two-legged creature with the fire-stick, then follow me and do just as I do."

The dog was very near now. In fact, he had his nose in the brambles and was standing as still as if turned to stone, one of his fore feet lifted and pointing straight at them. No one moved. Presently Tommy heard heavy steps, and, looking through the brambles, saw the great two-legged creature of whom Thunderer had told him.

"Now!" cried Thunderer. "Do as I do!" With a great roar of wings he burst out of the tangle on the opposite side from where the hunter was, and flying low, so as to keep the brambles between himself and the hunter, swerved sharply to the left to put a tree between them, and then flew like a bullet straight into the Green Forest where the trees were thickest, skilfully dodging the great trunks, and at last at a safe distance sailing up over the tops to take to the ground on the other side of a hill and there run swiftly for a way. Tommy followed closely, doing exactly as Thunderer did. Even as he swerved behind the first tree, he heard a terrible double roar behind him and the sharp whistle of things which cut through the leaves around him and struck the tree behind him. One even nipped a brown feather from his back. He was terribly frightened, but he was unhurt as he joined Thunderer behind the hill.

"Now you know what the greatest danger is," said Thunderer. "Never fly until you know just where the hunter is, and then fly back of a bush or a tree, the bigger the better, or drop over the edge of a bank if there is one. Make as much noise as you can when you get up. It may startle the hunter so that he cannot point his fire-stick straight. If he has no dog, it is sometimes best to lie still until he has passed and then fly silently. If there is no tree or other cover near enough when you first see the dog, run swiftly until you reach a place where it will be safe to take wing."

For the next few weeks it seemed as if from daylight to dark the woods were filled with dogs and hunters, and Tommy knew no hour of peace and security until the coming of night. Many a dreadful tragedy did Tommy see when companions, less cunning than old Thunderer, were stricken in mid-air and fell lifeless to the ground. But he, learning quickly and doing as Thunderer did, escaped unharmed.

At last the law, of which Tommy knew nothing, put an end to the murder of the innocents, and for another year the greatest danger was over. But now came a new danger. It was the month of madness. Tommy and all his companions were seized with an irresistible desire to fly aimlessly, blindly, sometimes in the darkness of night, they knew not where. And in this mad flight some met death, breaking their necks against buildings and against telegraph wires. Where he went or what he did during this period of madness, Tommy never knew; but when it left him as abruptly as it had come, he found himself in the street of a village.

Tommy knew no hour of peace and security. *Page 145.*

With swift strong wings he shot into the air and headed straight back for the dear Green Forest, now no longer green save where the hemlocks and pines grew. Once back there, he took up the old life and was happy, for he felt himself a match for any foe. The days grew shorter and the cold increased. There were still seeds and acorns and some berries, but with the coming of the snow these became more and more scarce and Tommy was obliged to resort to catkins and buds on the trees. Between his toes there grew little horny projectiles, which were his snowshoes and enabled him to get about on the snow without sinking in. He learned to dive into the deep soft snow for warmth and safety. Once he was nearly trapped there. A hard crust formed in the night and, when morning came, Tommy had hard work to break out.

So the long winter wore away and spring came with all its gladness. Tommy was fully as big as old Thunderer now and just as handsome, and he began to take pride in his appearance and to strut. One day he came to an old log, and, jumping up on it, strutted back and forth proudly with his fan-like tail spread its fullest and his broad ruff raised. Then he heard the long rolling thunder of another grouse drumming. Instantly he began to beat his wings against the air, not as in flying, but with a more downward motion, and to his great delight there rolled from under them that same thunder. Slowly he beat at first and then faster and faster, until he was forced to stop for breath. He was drumming! Then he listened for a reply.

Drum—drum—drum—drum—drum, drum, drum, dr-r-r-r-r-rum. Tommy's eyes flew open. He was sitting on the old wishing-stone on the edge of the Green Meadows. For a minute he blinked in confusion. Then, from over in the Green Forest, came that sound like distant thunder, *drum—drum—drum—drum—drum, drum, drum, dr-r-r-r-r-rum.*

"It's ol' Thunderer again on that beech log!" cried Tommy. "And now I know how he does it. He just beats the air. I know, because I've done it myself. Geewhilikens, I'm glad I'm not really a partridge! Bet I'll never hunt one after this, or let anybody else if I can help it. Ain't this old wishing-stone the dandy place to learn things, though! I guess the only way of really knowing how the critters live and feel is by being one of 'em. Somehow it makes things look all different. Just listen to ol' Thunderer drum! I know now just how fine he feels. I'm going to get Father to put up a sign and stop all shooting in our part of the Green Forest next fall, and then there won't be any greatest danger there."

And Tommy, whistling merrily, started for home.

IX
What Happened when Tommy Became a Mink

IT was not often that Tommy caught so much as a glimpse of Billy Mink; and every time he did, he had the feeling that he had been smart, very smart indeed. The funny thing is that this feeling annoyed Tommy. Yes, it did. It annoyed him because it seemed so very foolish to think that there was anything smart in just *seeing* Billy Mink. And yet every time he did see him, he had the feeling that he had really done something out of the usual.

Little by little, he realized that it was because Billy Mink himself is so smart, and manages to keep out of sight so much of the time, that just seeing him once in a while gave him the feeling of being smarter than Billy. At the same time, he was never quite sure that Billy didn't intend to be seen. Somehow that little brown-coated scamp always seemed to be playing with him. He would appear so suddenly that Tommy never could tell just where he came from. And he would disappear quite as quickly. Tommy never could tell where he went. He just vanished, that was all. It was this that made Tommy feel that he had been smart to see him at all.

Now Tommy had been acquainted with Billy Mink for a long time. That is to say, he had known Billy by sight. More than that, he had tried to trap Billy, and in trying to trap him he had learned some of Billy's ways. In fact, Tommy had spent a great deal of time trying to catch Billy. You see, he wanted that little brown fur coat of Billy's because he could sell it. But it was very clear that Billy wanted that little fur coat himself to wear, and also that he knew all about traps. So Billy still wore his coat, and Tommy had taken up his traps and put them away with a sigh for the money which he had hoped that that coat would bring him, and with a determination that, when cold weather should come again, he would get it. You see it was summer now, and the little fur coat was of no value then save to Billy himself.

In truth, Tommy would have forgotten all about it until autumn came again had not Billy suddenly popped out in front of him that very morning, while Tommy was trying to catch a trout in a certain quiet pool in the Laughing Brook deep in the Green Forest. Tommy had been sitting perfectly still, like a good fisherman that he was, not making the tiniest sound, when he just seemed to feel two eyes fixed on him. Very, very slowly Tommy turned his head. He did it so slowly that it almost seemed as if he didn't move it at all. But careful as he was, he had no more than a bare glimpse of a little brown animal, who disappeared as by magic.

"It's that mink," thought Tommy, and continued to stare at the spot where he had last seen Billy. The rustle of a leaf almost behind him caused him to forget and to turn quickly. Again he had just a glimpse of something brown. Then it was gone. Where, he hadn't the least idea. It was gone, that was all.

Tommy forgot all about trout. It was more fun to try to get a good look at Billy Mink and to see what he was doing and where he was going. Tommy remembered all that he had been taught or had read about how to act when trying to watch his little wild neighbors and he did the best he could, but all he got was a fleeting glimpse now and then which was most tantalizing. At last he gave up and reeled in his fish-line. Then he started for home. All the way he kept thinking of Billy Mink. He couldn't get Billy out of his head.

Little by little he realized how, when all was said and done, he didn't know anything about Billy. That is, he didn't really *know*—he just guessed at things.

"And here he is one of my neighbors," thought Tommy. "I know a great deal about Peter Rabbit, and Chatterer the Red Squirrel, and Reddy Fox, and a lot of others, but I don't know anything about Billy Mink, and he's too smart to let me find out. Huh! he needn't be so secret about everything. I ain't going to hurt him."

Then into Tommy's head crept a guilty remembrance of those traps. A little flush crept into Tommy's face. "Anyway, I ain't going to hurt him *now*," he added.

By this time he had reached the great gray stone on the edge of the Green Meadows, the wishing-stone. Just as a matter of course he sat down on the edge of it. He never could get by without sitting down on it. It was a very beautiful scene that stretched out before Tommy, but, though he seemed to be gazing out at it, he didn't see it at all. He was looking through unseeing eyes. The fact is, he was too busy thinking, and his thoughts were all of Billy Mink. It must be great fun to be able to go and come any hour of the day or night, and to be so nimble and smart.

"I wish I were a mink," said Tommy, slowly and very earnestly.

Of course you know what happened then. The same thing happened that had happened so many times before on the old wishing-stone. Tommy was the very thing he had wished to be. He was a mink. Yes, sir, Tommy was a tiny furry little fellow, with brothers and sisters and the nicest little home, in a hollow log hidden among bulrushes, close by the Laughing Brook and with a big pile of brush near it. Indeed, one end of the old log was under the brush-pile. That made the very safest kind of a playground for the little minks. It was there that Mother Mink gave them their first lessons in a game called "Now-you-see-me-now-you-don't." They thought they were just playing, but all the time they were learning something that would be most important and useful to them when they were older.

Tommy was very quick to learn and just as quick in his movements, so that it wasn't long before he could out-run, out-dodge, and out-hide any of his companions, and Mother Mink began to pay special attention to his education. She was proud of him, and because she was proud of him she intended to teach him all the mink lore which she knew. So Tommy was the first of the family to be taken fishing. Ever since he and his brothers and sisters had been big enough to eat solid food, they had had fish as a part of their bill of fare, and there was nothing that Tommy liked better. Where they came from, he had never bothered to ask. All he cared about was the eating of them. But now he was actually going to catch some, and he felt very important as he glided along behind his mother.

Presently they came to a dark deep pool in the Laughing Brook. Mrs. Mink peered into its depths. There was the glint of something silvery down there in the brown water. In a flash Mrs. Mink had disappeared in the pool, entering the water so smoothly as to hardly make a splash. For a moment Tommy saw her dark form moving swiftly, then he lost it. His little eyes blazed with eagerness and excitement as he watched. Ha! What was that? There was something moving under water on the other side of the pool. Then out popped the brown head of Mrs. Mink and in her teeth was a fat trout. Tommy's mouth watered at the sight. What a feast he would have!

Out popped the brown head of Mrs. Mink and
in her teeth was a fat trout. *Page 153.*

But instead of bringing the fish to him, Mrs. Mink climbed out on the opposite bank and disappeared in the brush there. Tommy swallowed hard with disappointment. Could it be that he wasn't to have any of it after all? In a few minutes Mrs. Mink was back again, but there was no sign of the fish. Then Tommy knew that she had hidden it, and for just a minute a wicked thought popped into his head. He would swim across and hunt for it. But Mother Mink didn't give him a chance. Though Tommy didn't see it, there was a twinkle in her eyes as she said,

"Now you have seen how easy it is to catch a fish, I shall expect you to catch all you eat hereafter. Come along with me to the next pool and show me how well you have learned your lesson."

She led the way down the Laughing Brook, and presently they came to another little brown pool. Eagerly Tommy peered into it. At first he saw nothing. Then, almost under him, he discovered a fat trout lazily watching for a good meal to come along. With a great splash Tommy dived into the pool. For just a second he closed his eyes as he struck the water. When he opened them, the trout was nowhere to be seen. Tommy looked very crestfallen and foolish as he crawled up on the bank, where Mother Mink was laughing at him.

"How do you expect to catch fish when you splash like that?" she asked. Tommy didn't know, so he said nothing. "Now you come with me and practise on little fish first," she continued, and led him to a shallow pool in which a school of minnows were at play. Now Tommy was particularly fond of trout, as all Mink are, and he was inclined to turn up his nose at minnows. But he wisely held his tongue and prepared to show that he had learned his lesson. This time he slipped into the water quietly and then made a swift dash at the nearest minnow. He missed it quite as Mother Mink had expected he would, but now his dander was up. He would catch one of those minnows if it took him all the rest of the day! Three times he tried and missed, but the fourth time his sharp little teeth closed on a finny victim and he proudly swam ashore with the fish.

"Things you catch yourself always taste best," said Mother Mink. "Now we'll go over on the meadows and catch some mice."

Tommy scowled. "I want to catch some more fish," said he.

"Not the least bit of use for you to try," retorted Mother Mink. "Don't you see that you have frightened those minnows so that they have left the pool? Besides, it is time that you learned to hunt as well as fish, and you'll find it is just as much fun."

Tommy doubted it, but he obediently trotted along at the heels of Mother Mink out onto the Green Meadows. Presently they came to a tiny little path through the meadow grasses. Mother Mink sniffed in it and Tommy did the same. There was the odor of meadow-mouse, and once more Tommy's mouth watered. He quite forgot about the fish. Mother Mink darted ahead and presently Tommy heard a faint squeak. He hurried forward to find Mother Mink with a fat meadow-mouse. Tommy smacked his lips, but she took no notice. Instead, she calmly ate the meadow-mouse herself.

Tommy didn't need to be told that if he wanted meadow-mouse he would have to catch one for himself. With a little angry toss of his head he trotted off along the little path. Presently he came to another. His nose told him a meadow-mouse had been along that way very recently. With his nose to the ground he began to run. Other little paths branched off from the one he was in. Tommy paid no attention to them until suddenly he realized that he no longer smelled meadow-mouse. He kept on a little farther, hoping that he would find that entrancing smell again. But he didn't, so he stopped to consider. Then he turned and ran back, keeping his nose to the ground. So he came to one of those little branch paths and there he caught the smell of meadow-mouse again. He turned into the little branch path and the smell grew stronger. He ran faster. Then his quick ears caught the sound of scurrying feet ahead of him. He darted along, and there, running for his life, was a fat meadow-mouse. Half a dozen bounds brought Tommy up with him, whereupon the mouse turned to fight. Now the mouse was big and a veteran, and Tommy was only a youngster. It was his first fight. For just a second he paused at the sight of the sharp

The mouse turned to fight. *Page 157.*

little teeth confronting him. Then he sprang into his first fight. The fierce lust of battle filled him. His eyes blazed red. There was a short sharp struggle and then the mouse went limp and lifeless. Very proudly Tommy dragged it out to where Mother Mink was waiting. She would have picked it up and carried it easily, but Tommy wasn't big enough for that.

After that Tommy went hunting or fishing every day. Sometimes the whole family went, and such fun as they would have! One day they would hunt frogs around the edge of the Smiling Pool. Again they would visit a swamp and dig out worms and insects. But best of all they liked to hunt the meadow-mice. So the long summer wore away and the family kept together. But as the cool weather of the fall came, Tommy grew more and more restless. He wanted to see the Great World. Sometimes he would go off and be gone two or three days at a time. Then one day he bade the old home good-by forever, though he didn't know it at the time. He simply started off, following the Laughing Brook to the Great River, in search of adventure, and in the joy of exploring new fields he forgot all about home.

He was a fine big fellow by this time and very smart in the ways of the Mink world. Life was just a grand holiday. He hunted or fished when he was hungry, and when he was tired he curled up in the nearest hiding-place and slept. Sometimes it was in a hollow log or stump. Again it was in an old rock-pile or under a heap of brush. When he had slept enough, he was off again on his travels, and it made no difference to him whether it was night or day. He just ate when he pleased, slept when he pleased, and wandered on where and when he pleased. He was afraid of no one. Once in a while a fox would try to catch him or a fierce hawk would swoop at him, but Tommy would only dodge like a flash, and laugh as he ducked into some hole or other hiding-place. He had learned that quickness of movement often is more than a match for mere size and strength. So he was not afraid of any of his neighbors, for those he was not strong enough to fight he was clever enough to elude.

He could run swiftly, climb like a squirrel, and swim like a fish. Because he was so slim, he could slip into all kinds of interesting holes and dark corners, and explore stone and brush piles. In fact he could go almost anywhere he pleased. His nose was as keen as that of a dog. He was always testing the air or sniffing at the ground for the odor of other little people who had passed that way. When he was hungry and ran across the trail of some one he fancied, he would follow it just as Bowser the Hound follows the trail of Reddy Fox. Sometimes he would follow the trail of Reddy himself, just to see what he was doing.

For the most part he kept near water. He dearly loved to explore a brook, running along beside it, swimming the pools, investigating every hole in the banks and the piles of drift stuff. When he was

When he was feeling lazy, he would catch a frog. *Page 162*.

feeling lazy and there were no fish handy, he would catch a frog or two, or a couple of pollywogs, or a crayfish. Occasionally he would leave the low land and the water for the high land and hunt rabbits and grouse. Sometimes he surprised other ground birds. Once he visited a farmyard and, slipping into the hen-house at night, killed three fat hens. Of course he could not eat the whole of even one.

Tommy asked no favors of any one. His was a happy, care-free life. To be sure he had few friends save among his own kind, but he didn't mind this. He rather enjoyed the fact that all who were smaller, and some who were larger than he, feared him. He was lithe and strong and wonderfully quick. Fighting was a joy. It was this as much as anything that led him into a fight with a big muskrat, much bigger than himself. The muskrat was stout, and his great teeth looked dangerous. But he was slow and clumsy in his movements compared with Tommy, and, though he was full of courage and fought hard, the battle was not long. After that Tommy hunted muskrats whenever the notion seized him.

Winter came, but Tommy minded it not at all. His thick fur coat kept him warm, and the air was like tonic in his veins. It was good to be alive. He hunted rabbits in the snow. He caught fish at spring-holes in the ice. He traveled long distances under the ice, running along the edge of the water where it had fallen away from the frozen crust, swimming when he had to, investigating muskrat holes, and now and then surprising the tenant. Unlike his small cousin, Shadow the Weasel, he seldom hunted and killed just for the fun of killing. Sometimes, when fishing was especially good and he caught more than he could use, he would hide them away against a day of need. In killing, the mink is simply obeying the law of Old Mother Nature, for she has given him flesh-eating teeth, and without meat he could not live. In this respect he is no worse than man, for man kills to live.

For the most of the time, Tommy was just a happy-go-lucky traveler, who delighted in exploring new places and who saw more of the Great World than most of his neighbors. The weather never bothered him. He liked the sun, but he would just as soon travel in the rain. When a fierce snow-storm raged, he traveled under the ice along the bed of the nearest brook or river. It was just the life he had dreamed of as a boy. He was an adventurer, a freebooter, and all the world was his. He had no work. He had no fear, for as yet he had not encountered man. Hooty the Owl by night and certain of the big hawks by day were all he had to watch out for, and these he did not really fear, for he felt himself too smart for them.

But at last he did learn fear. It came to him when he discovered another Mink fast in a trap. He didn't understand those strange jaws which bit into the flesh and held and yet were not alive. He hid near by and watched, and he saw a great two-legged creature come and take the mink away. Then, cautiously,

He hid near by and watched, and saw a great two-legged creature come. *Page 163.*

Tommy investigated. He caught the odor of the man scent, and a little chill of fear ran down his backbone.

But in spite of all his care there came a fateful day. He was running along a brook in shallow water when snap! from the bottom of the brook itself the dreadful jaws sprang up and caught him by a leg. There had been no smell of man to give him warning, for the running water had carried it away. Tommy gave a little shriek as he felt the dreadful thing, and then— he was just Tommy, sitting on the wishing-stone.

He stared thoughtfully over at the Green Forest. Then he shuddered. You see he remembered just how he had felt when that trap had snapped on his leg. "I don't want your fur coat, Billy Mink," said he, just as if Billy could hear him. "If it wasn't for traps, you surely would enjoy life. Just the same I wouldn't trade places with you, not even if I do have to hoe corn just when I want to go swimming!"

And with this, Tommy started for home and the hoe, and somehow the task didn't look so very dreadful after all.

X

The Pleasures and Troubles of Bobby Coon

TOMMY was trudging down to the corn-field, and his freckled face was rather sober. At least it was sober for him, considering why he was on his way to the corn-field. It wasn't to work. If it had been, his sober look would have been quite easy to understand. The fact is, Tommy was going on an errand that once would have filled him with joy and sent him whistling all the way.

"Coons are raising mischief down in the corn! You'd better get your traps out and see if you can catch the thieving little rascals. Go down and look the ground over, and see what you think," his father had said to him at noon, that day.

So here he was on his way to look for signs of Bobby Coon, and, if the truth were known, actually hoping that he wouldn't find them! There had been a time when he would have been all excitement over his quest, and eager to find the tell-tale tracks where Bobby Coon went into and out of the corn-field. Then he would have hurried home for his traps in great glee, or instead would have planned to watch with his gun for the marauder that very night.

But now he had no such feelings. Somehow, he had come to regard his little wild neighbors in a wholly different light. He no longer desired to do them harm. Ever since he had begun to learn what their real lives were like, by wishing himself one of them as he sat on the old wishing-stone, he had cared less and less to hunt and frighten them and more and more to try to make friends with them. His teacher would have said that he had a "sympathetic understanding" of them, and then probably would have had to explain to Tommy what that meant—that he knew just how they felt and had learned to look at things from their point of view. And it was true. He had put away his gun and traps. He no longer desired to kill. He liked to hunt for these little wild people as much as ever, perhaps more, but it was in order to make friends with them, and to find out more about their ways and habits, instead of to kill them.

So it was that he didn't like his present errand. On the brow of the hill that overlooked the corn-field he stopped for a minute to look down on the broad acres of long-leaved stalks standing row on row, row on row, like a well drilled army. He thought of the long hours he had spent among them toiling with his hoe in the hot sunshine when the swimming-hole was calling to him, and a sudden sense of pride swept over him. The great sturdy plants no longer needed his hoe to keep the weeds down. The ears had filled out and were in the milk now.

"Seems as if we could spare what little a coon wants," muttered Tommy, as he gazed down on the field. "Of course, if there is a whole family of 'em, something's got to be done, but I don't believe one coon can eat enough to do much harm. Dad promised me a share in the crop, when it's harvested, to pay for my work. 'Tain't likely to be very much, and goodness knows I want every penny of it; but I guess, if that coon ain't doing too much damage, I can pay for it."

Tommy's face lighted up at the idea. It was going to take self-denial on his part, but it was a way out. The thought chased the soberness from his face and put a spring into his hitherto reluctant steps. He went at once to that part of the corn-field nearest the Green Forest. It did not take him long to discover the evidences that a raccoon, or perhaps more than one, had been taking toll. Here a stalk less sturdy than its neighbors had been pulled down, the husks stripped from the ears, and a few mouthfuls of the milky grains taken. There a stalk had been climbed and an ear stripped and bitten into.

"Wasteful little beggar!" muttered Tommy. "Why can't you be content to take an ear at a time and clean it up? Then there would be no kick coming. Dad wouldn't mind if you filled your little tummy every night, if you didn't spoil ten times as much as you eat. Ha! here are your tracks. Now we'll see where you come in."

Except for the sharp tips of the toes, the tracks were not unlike the print of a tiny hand, and there was no mistaking them for the tracks of any other animal. Tommy studied them until he was sure that all were made by one raccoon, and he was convinced that he had but a single foe to deal with. At length he found the place where the animal was in the habit of entering the field. There was just the suggestion of a path through the grass in the direction of the Green Forest. It was very clear that Bobby Coon came and went regularly that way, and of course this was the place to set a trap. Tommy's face clouded again at the thought.

"I believe I'll go up to the old wishing-stone and think it out," he muttered.

So he headed for the familiar old wishing-stone that overlooked the Green Meadows and the corn-field, and was not so very far from the Green Forest; and when he reached it, he sat down. It is doubtful if Tommy ever got past that old stone without sitting down on it. This time he had no intention of wishing himself into anything, and yet hardly had he sat down when he did. You see his thoughts were all of Bobby Coon, and so, without stopping to think where he was, he said to no one in particular: "There are some things I want to know about raccoons. I wish I could be one long enough to find out."

Tommy's wish had come true. He was no longer Tommy the boy, but Tommy the coon. He was a thick-set, rather clumsy-looking gray-coated fellow, with a black-ringed tail and a black band across the eyes. His ears were sharp, and his face was not un-like that of Reddy Fox in its outline. His toes were long and bare; and when he walked, it was with his whole foot on the ground as a man does and as a bear does. In fact, although he didn't know it, he was own cousin to Buster Bear.

Tommy's home was a hollow tree with the entrance high up. Inside he had a comfortable bed, and there he spent his days sleeping away the long hours of sunshine. Night was the time he liked best to be abroad, and then he roamed far and wide without fear. Reddy Fox he was not afraid of at all. In fact there was no one he really feared but man, and in the darkness of the night he thought he need not even fear him. Tommy's hollow tree was in a swamp through which flowed a brook, and it was Tommy's delight to explore this brook, sometimes up, sometimes down. In it were fish to be caught, and Tommy as a boy never delighted in fishing more than did Tommy as a coon. On moonlight nights he would steal softly up to a quiet pool and, on the very edge of it, possess himself in patience, as a good fisherman should. Presently a careless fish would swim within reach. A swift scoop with a black little paw with five sharp little hooks extended—and the fish would be high and dry on the shore. It was great fun.

Sometimes he would visit marshy places where the frogs were making the night noisy with a mighty chorus. This was the easiest kind of hunting. He had only to locate the spot from which one of those voices issued, steal softly up, and there was one less singer, though the voice would hardly be missed

In the brook were fish to be caught. *Page 170.*

in the great chorus. Occasionally he would take a hint from Jerry Muskrat and, where the water was very shallow, dig out a few mussels or fresh-water clams.

At other times, just by way of varying his bill of fare, he would go hunting. This was less certain of results but exciting; and when successful, the reward was great. Especially was this so in the nesting season, and many a good meal of eggs did Tommy have, to say nothing of tender young birds. Occasionally he prowled through the tree-tops in hope of surprising a family of young squirrels in their sleep. None knew better than he that in the light of day he could not catch them; but at night, when they could not see and he could, it was another matter.

But fish, meat, and eggs were only a part of Tommy's diet. Fruit, berries, and nuts in their season were quite as much to his liking, not to mention certain tender roots. One day, quite by chance while he was exploring a hollow tree, he discovered that it already had tenants and that they were makers of the most delicious sweets he ever had tasted. In short, he almost made himself sick on wild honey, his long hair protecting him from the little lances of the bees. After that he kept a sharp eye out for sweets and so discovered that bumble-bees make their nests in the ground; and that while they contained a scant supply of honey, there was enough as a rule to make it worth while to dig them open.

Once in a while, he would be discovered. *Page 174.*

So Tommy grew fat and lazy. There was plenty to eat without working very hard for it, and he shuffled about in the Green Forest and along the Laughing Brook, eating whatever tempted him and having a good time generally. He dearly loved to play along the edge of the water and was as tickled as a child with anything bright and shiny. Once he found a bit of tin shining in the moonlight and spent most of the remainder of that night playing with it. About one thing he was very particular. If he had meat of any kind and there was water near, he always washed it carefully before eating. In fact Tommy was very neat. It was born in him.

Sometimes daylight caught him far from his hollow tree. Then he would look for an old nest of a hawk or crow and curl up in it to sleep the day away. If none was handy and he could find no hollow tree or stump, he would climb a big tree and stretch himself flat along one of the big limbs and there sleep until the Black Shadows came creeping through the Green Forest. Once in a while he would be discovered by the sharp eyes of Sammy Jay or Blacky the Crow, and then life would be made miserable for him until he would be glad to wake up and seek some hiding-place where they could not see him. It was for this reason chiefly that he always tried to get back to his own snug den by the time jolly, round, red Mr. Sun shook his rosy blankets off and began his daily climb up in the blue, blue sky.

One night he met Bobby Coon himself.

One night he met Bobby Coon himself. *Page 174*.

"Where do you live?" asked Tommy.

"Over on the Mountain," replied Bobby.

"In a hollow tree?" asked Tommy.

"No. Oh, my, no!" replied Bobby. "I've got the nicest den in a ledge of rock. No more hollow trees for me."

"Why not?" demanded Tommy.

"They aren't safe," retorted Bobby. "I used to live in a hollow tree, but I've learned better. I guess you've never been hunted. When you've been nearly choked to death by smoke in your hollow tree, or had it cut down with you in it and barely escaped by the skin of your teeth, you won't think so much of hollow trees. Give me a good rocky den every time."

"But where does the smoke come from, and why should my hollow tree be cut down?" asked Tommy, to whom this was all new and very strange.

"Hunters," replied Bobby briefly. "You wait until the cool weather comes and you'll find out what I mean."

"But who are the hunters and what do they hunt us for?" persisted Tommy.

"My, but you are innocent!" retorted Bobby. "They are those two-legged creatures called men, and I don't know what they hunt us for. They just do, that's all. They seem to think it's fun. I wish one of them would have to fight for *his* life. Perhaps he wouldn't see so much fun in it then. It was last fall that they drove me out of my hollow tree, and they pretty nearly got me, too. But they won't do it this year! You take my advice and get a den in the rocks. Then you can laugh at them."

"But what will they hunt me for? I haven't done them any harm," persisted Tommy.

"That doesn't have anything to do with it," retorted Bobby. "They do it for *fun*. Have you tried the corn yet? It's perfectly delicious. Come on and we'll have a feast."

Now of course Tommy was ready for a feast. The very thought of it put everything else out of his head. He shuffled along behind Bobby Coon through the Green Forest, across a little stretch of meadow, and under the bars of a fence into a corn-field. For a minute he sat and watched Bobby. It was Tommy's first visit to a corn-field and he didn't know just what to do. But Bobby did. Oh, yes, Bobby did. He stood up on his hind legs and pulled one of the more slender stalks down until he could get at the lowest ear. Then he stripped off the husk and took a huge bite of the tender milky kernels.

"Um-m-m," said Bobby Coon, and took another.

Tommy waited no longer. He found a stalk for himself, and two minutes later he was stuffing himself with the most delicious meal he ever had tasted. At least he thought so then. He forgot all about dens and hunters. He had no thought for anything but the feast before him. Here was plenty and to spare. He dropped the ear he was eating and climbed a big stalk to strip another ear. The first one was good but

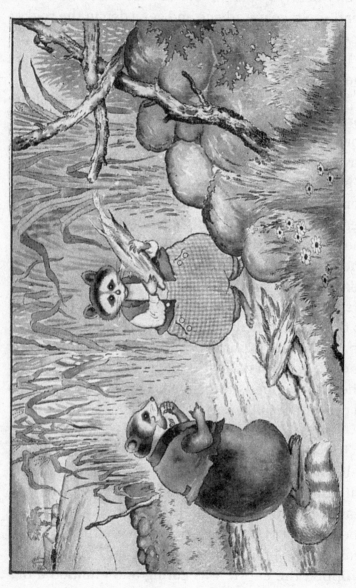

It was Tommy's first visit to a corn-field. *Page 177.*

this one was better. Perhaps a third would be better still. So he sampled a third. The moon flooded the corn-field with silvery light. It was just the kind of a night that all raccoons love, and in that field of plenty Bobby and Tommy were perfectly happy. They did not know that they were in mischief. How should they? The corn was no more than other green things growing of which they were free to help themselves. So they wandered about, taking here a bite and there a bite and wasting many times as much as they ate.

Suddenly, in the midst of their good time, there sounded the yelp of a dog, and there was something about it that sent a chill of fright along Tommy's backbone. It was an excited and joyous yelp, and yet there was something threatening in it. It was followed by another yelp, and then another, each more excited than the others, and then it broke into a full-throated roar in which there was something fierce and terrifying. It was coming nearer through the corn. Tommy looked over to where he had last seen Bobby Coon. He wasn't there, but a rustling of the corn-stalks beyond told him that Bobby was running, running for his life.

Tommy was in a panic. He never had had to run for his life before. Where should he go? To the Green Forest of course, where there were trees to climb. In a tree he would be safe. Then he heard another sound, the shout of a man. He remembered what

Bobby Coon had said about trees and a new fear took possession of him. While he still hesitated, the dog passed, only a few yards away in the corn. Tommy heard the rustle of the stalks and the roar of his savage voice. And then suddenly he knew that the dog was not after him. He was following the tracks of Bobby Coon.

Swiftly Tommy stole through the corn and ran across the bit of meadow, his heart in his mouth, to the great black bulk of the Green Forest. He ran swiftly, surprisingly so for such a clumsy-looking fellow. How friendly the tall trees looked! They seemed to promise safety. It was hard to believe that Bobby Coon was right and that they did not. He kept on, nor stopped until he was in his own hollow tree. The voice of the dog came to him, growing fainter and fainter in the direction of the mountain, and finally ceased altogether. He wondered if Bobby reached his den and was safe.

Of one thing Tommy was certain; that corn-field was no place for him. So he kept away from it and tried not to think of how good that milky corn had tasted. So the summer passed and the fall came with falling leaves and sharp frosty nights. They gave Tommy even more of an appetite, though there had been nothing the matter with that before. He grew fatter and fatter so that it made him puff to run. Unknown to him, Old Mother Nature was preparing him for the long winter sleep. By this time the memory of the dog and of what Bobby Coon had said about hollow trees had almost dropped from his mind. He was concerned over nothing but filling his stomach and enjoying those frosty moonlight nights. He interfered with no one and no one interfered with him.

One night he had gone down to the Laughing Brook, fishing. Without warning, there broke out on the still air the horrid sound of that yelping dog. Tommy listened for just a minute. This time it was *his* tracks that dog was following. There could be no doubt about it. Tommy turned and ran swiftly. But he was fat and heavy, and he could hear the dog gaining rapidly. Straight for his hollow tree fled Tommy, and even as he reached it the dog was almost at his heels. Up the tree scrambled Tommy and, from the safe vantage of a big limb which was the threshold of his home, he looked down. The dog was leaping up against the base of the tree excitedly and his voice had changed. He was barking. A feeling of relief swept over Tommy. The dog could not climb; he was safe.

But presently there were new sounds in the Green Forest, the shouting of men. Lights twinkled and drew nearer. Staring down from the edge of his hole, Tommy saw eager, cruel faces looking up. With a terrible fear gripping his heart he crept down into his bed. Presently the tree shook with the jar of an ax. Blow followed blow. The tree vibrated to each blow and the vibrations passed through Tommy's body so that it shook, but it shook still more with a nameless and terrible fear.

At last there was a sharp cracking sound. Tommy felt himself falling through space. He remembered what Bobby Coon had told him, and he wondered if he would be lucky enough to escape as Bobby did. Then he shut his eyes tight, waiting for the crash when the tree should strike the ground.

When he opened his eyes, he was—just Tommy, sitting on the wishing-stone overlooking the Green Meadows. His face was wet with perspiration. Was it from the sun beating down upon him, or was it from the fear that had gripped him when that tree began to fall? A shudder ran over him at the memory. He looked over to the corn-field where he had found the tracks of Bobby Coon and the mischief he had wrought. What was he to do about it? Somehow his sympathy was strangely with Bobby.

"He doesn't know any better," muttered Tommy. "He thinks that corn belongs to him as much as to anybody else, and there isn't any reason why he shouldn't think so. It isn't fair to trap him or kill him for something he doesn't know he shouldn't do. If he just knew enough to eat what he wants and not waste so much, I guess there wouldn't be any trouble. He's just like a lot of folks who have so much they don't know what to do with it, only they know better than to waste it, and he doesn't. I know what I'll do. I'll take Bowser down there to-night and give him a scare. I'll give him such a scare that he won't dare come back until the corn is so hard he won't want it. That's what I'll do!

"My, it must be awful to think you're safe and then find you're trapped! I guess I won't ever hunt coons any more. I used to think it was fun, but I never thought how the coon must feel. Now I know and—and—well, a live coon is a lot more interesting than a dead one, anyway. Funny what I find out on this old wishing-stone. If I keep on, I won't want to hunt anything any more."

Tommy got up, stretched, began to whistle as if there was a load off his mind, and started for home, still whistling.

And his whistle was good to hear.

XI
Tommy Becomes a Furry Engineer

PADDY THE BEAVER lives in the Great Woods far from the dwelling-place of man. Often and often had Tommy wished that Paddy lived in the Green Forest near his home that he might make his acquaintance; for he had read many wonderful things about Paddy, and they were hard to believe.

"If I could see 'em for myself, just 'em with my own eyes I could believe; but so many things are written that are not true, that a feller don't know what to believe and what not to. A feller ought to *see* things to *know* that they are so," said Tommy, as he strolled down towards the big gray stone that overlooked the Green Meadows. "'Course it's easy enough to believe that beavers build houses. Muskrats do that. I know all about muskrats, and I s'pose a beaver's house is about the same thing as a muskrat's, only bigger and better; but how any critter can cut down a big tree, or build a dam, or dig a regular canal is more 'n I can understand without seeing for myself. I wish—"

Tommy didn't finish his wish. I suspect he was going to wish that he could go into the Great Woods and hunt for Paddy the Beaver. But he didn't finish his wish, because just then a new thought popped

184

into his head. You know how it is with thoughts. They just pop out from nowhere in the queerest way. It was so now with Tommy. He suddenly thought of the wishing-stone, the great gray stone just ahead of him, and he wondered, if he should sit down on it, if he could wish himself into a beaver. Always before, when he had wished himself into an animal or a bird, it was one of those with which he was familiar and had seen. This case was different. There were no beavers anywhere near where Tommy lived, and so he was a little doubtful. If he could wish himself into a beaver, why, he could wish himself into anything— a lion, or an elephant, or anything else—and learn about *all* the animals, no matter where they lived!

"Gee!" exclaimed Tommy, and there was a queer little catch in his breath, because, you know, it was such a great big idea. He stood still and slowly rubbed the bare toes of one foot up and down the other bare brown leg. "Gee!" he exclaimed again, and stared very hard at the wishing-stone. "'Twon't do any harm to try it, anyway," he added.

So he walked over to the wishing-stone and sat down. With his chin in his hand and his elbows on his knees he stared over at the Green Forest and tried to imagine that it was the Great Woods, where the only human beings ever seen were hunters, or trappers, or lumbermen, and where bears, and deer, and moose, and wolves lived, and where beavers built their homes, and made their ponds, and lived their lives far from the homes of men. As he stared, the Green Forest seemed to change to the Great Woods. "I wish," said he, slowly and dreamily, "I wish that I were a beaver."

He was no longer sitting on the wishing-stone. He was a young beaver with a waterproof fur coat, a broad flat tail and great chisel-like teeth in the front of his jaws, his tools. His home was in the heart of the Great Woods, where a broad, shallow brook sparkled and dimpled, and the sun, breaking through the tree-tops, kissed its ripples. In places it flowed swiftly, dancing and singing over stones and pebbles. Again it lingered in deep dark cool holes where the trout lay. Farther on, it loafed lazily through wild meadows where the deer delighted to come. But where Tommy was, it rested in little ponds, quiet, peaceful, in a dreamy quietness, where the very spirit of peace and happiness and contentment seemed to brood.

On one side of one of these little ponds was the house, a great house of sticks bound together with mud and turf, the house in which Tommy lived with others of his family. It was quite the finest beaver-house in all that region. But Tommy didn't think anything about that. It was summer now, the season of play, of having a good time without thought of work. It was the season of visiting and of exploration. In company with some of his relatives he made long journeys up and down the brook, and even across to other brooks on some of which were other beaver colonies and on some of which were no signs that beavers ever had worked there.

Tommy was a young beaver with a
waterproof fur coat. *Page 186.*

But when summer began to wane, Tommy found that life was not all a lazy holiday and that he was expected to work. The home settlement was rather crowded. There was danger that the food supply would not be sufficient for so many hungry beavers. So it was decided to establish a new settlement on one of the brooks which they had visited in their summer journey, and Tommy was one of a little company which, under the leadership of a wise old beaver, started forth on a still night to found the new colony. He led the way straight to one of the brooks on the banks of which grew many poplar trees, for you must know that the favorite food of beavers is the bark of aspens and poplars. It was very clear that this wise old leader had taken note during the summer of those trees and of the brook itself, for the very night of their arrival he chose a certain place in the brook and announced that there they would build their dam.

"Isn't it a great deal of work to build a dam?" asked Tommy, who knew nothing about dam-building, the dam at his old home having been built long before his time.

"It is. Yes, indeed, it certainly is," replied an old beaver. "You'll find it so before we get this dam built."

"Then what's the use of building it?" asked Tommy. "I don't see the use of a dam here anyway. There are places where the banks are steep enough and the

"Isn't it a great deal of work to build a dam?" *Page 188.*

water deep enough for splendid holes in which to live. Then all we've got to do is to go cut a tree when we are hungry. I'm sure I, for one, would much rather swim around and have a good time."

The other looked at him out of eyes that twinkled, and yet in a way to make Tommy feel uncomfortable. "You are young," said he, "and the prattle of young tongues is heedness. What would you do for food in winter when the brook is frozen? The young think only of to-day and the good times of to-day, and forget to prepare for the future. When you have learned to work, you will find that there is in life no pleasure so great as the pleasure of work well done. Now suppose you let us see what those teeth of yours are good for, and help cut these alders and haul them over to the place where the dam is to be."

Tommy had no reply ready, and so he set to work cutting young alders and willows as the rest were doing. These were floated or dragged down to the place chosen for the dam, where the water was very shallow, and were laid side by side with the big ends pointing up stream. Turf, and stones, and mud were piled on the brushy ends to keep them in place. So the foundations of the dam were laid from bank to bank. Then more poles were laid on top, and more turf and mud. Short sticks were wedged in between and helped to hold the long sticks in place. Tommy grew tired of working, but no one else stopped and he was ashamed to.

One of his companions cut a big poplar and others helped him trim off the branches. This was for food; and when the branches and trunk had been stripped of bark, they were floated down to the new dam and worked into it, the trunk being cut into lengths which could be managed easily. Thus nothing went to waste. So all through the stilly night they worked, and, when the day broke, they sought the deep water and certain holes under the banks wherein to rest. But before he left the dam, the wise old leader examined the work all over to make sure that it was right.

When the first shadows crept forth late the next afternoon, the old leader was the first back on the work. One by one the others joined him, and another night of labor had begun. Some cut trees and saplings, some hauled them to the dam, and some dug up turf and mud and piled it on the dam. There was no talking. Everybody was too busy to talk. Most of Tommy's companions had helped build dams before and knew just what to do. Tommy asked no questions, but did as the others did. Slowly the dam grew higher, and Tommy noticed that the brook was spreading out into a pool; for the water came down faster than it could work its way through that pile of poles and brush. Twigs, and leaves, and grass floated down from the places higher up where the beavers were at work, and, when these reached the dam, they were carried in among the sticks by the water

Some cut trees and saplings, some hauled
them to the dam. *Page 191.*

and lodged there, helping to fill up the holes and hold the water back.

As night after night the dam grew higher and the pool behind it grew broader and deeper, Tommy began to take pride in his work. He no longer thought of play but was as eager as the others to complete the dam. The stars looked down from the soft sky and twinkled as they saw the busy workers. At last the dam was completed, for the time being, at least. Very thoroughly the wise old leader went all over it, inspecting it from end to end; and when he was satisfied, he led his band to one side of the little pond formed by the dam, and there he chose a site for the house wherein they would spend the winter.

First a platform of sticks, and mud, and turf was built until it was a few inches above the water. Then began the raising of the walls: a framework of poles or long sticks first, and on these a mass of brush and turf until the walls were three feet thick and so solid that Jack Frost would find it quite useless to try to get inside. The roof was in the shape of a rough dome and at the top was comparatively thin; here little or no mud was used, so that there were tiny air-holes, for, like all other warm-blooded animals, a beaver must breathe.

Within, was a comfortable room of which the platform was the floor. From this, two burrows, or tunnels, led down on the deep-water side, one of these being on a gradual incline, that food sticks might the easier be dragged in. The entrances to both were at the very bottom of the pond, where there would be no danger of them being closed by ice when the pond should freeze in winter. These were the only entrances, so that no foe could reach them unless he were able to swim under water, and there were no such swimmers whom they had cause to fear.

When the house was finished, Tommy thought that their labors would be at an end; and he was almost sorry, for he had learned to love work. But no sooner was the house completed than all the beavers went lumbering. Yes, sir, that is just what they did. They went lumbering just as men do, only they cut the trees for food instead of for boards. They began at the edge of a little grove of poplars to which the pond now nearly extended. Sitting on his haunches with his broad tail for a seat or a prop, as his fancy pleased, each little woodman grasped the tree with his hands and bit into the trunk, a bite above and a bite below, and then with his teeth pried out the chip between the two bites, exactly as a man with an ax would cut. It was slow hard work cutting out a chip at a time in this way, but sooner or later the tree would begin to sway. A bite or two more, and it would begin to topple over. Then the little workman would thud the ground sharply with his tail to warn his neighbors to get out of the way, and he himself would scamper to a place of safety while the tree came crashing down. Tommy dearly loved to see and hear those trees come crashing to the ground.

No sooner was a tree down than they trimmed off the branches and cut the trunk into short lengths. These logs they rolled into the water, where, with the larger branches, they were floated out to deep water close by the house and there sunk to the bottom. What for? Tommy didn't have to be told. This was the beginning of their food-pile for the winter.

So the days slipped away and the great food-pile grew in the pond. With such busy workers it did not take long to cut all the trees close by the pond. The farther away from the water they got, the greater the labor of dragging and rolling the logs, and also the greater the danger from lurking enemies. In the water they felt wholly safe, but on land they had to be always on the watch for wolves, and bears, and lynxes.

When they had reached the limit of safety, the wise old leader called a halt to tree cutting and set them all to digging. And what do you think it was they were digging? Why, a canal! It was easier and safer to lead the water from the pond to the place where the trees grew than to get the logs over land to the pond. So they dug a ditch, or canal, about two and a half feet wide and a foot and a half deep, piling the mud up on the banks, until at last it reached the place where they could cut the trees, and roll the logs into the canal, and so float them out to the pond. Then the cutting began again.

Tommy was happy. Never had he been more happy. There was something wonderfully satisfying in just looking at the results of their labor and in feeling that he had had a part in it all. Yet his life was not all labor without excitement. Indeed, it was far from it. Had Tommy the Beaver been able to remember what as Tommy the Boy he had read, he would have felt that he was just like those hardy pioneers who built their homes in the wilderness. Always, in that great still wilderness, death with padded feet, and cruel teeth, and hungry eyes sought to steal upon the beavers. So always as they worked, especially when on the land, they were prepared to rush for safety at the first warning. Never for a minute did they cease to keep guard, testing every breath of air with wonderfully sensitive noses, and listening with hardly less wonderful ears. On nose and ears the safety of a beaver almost wholly depends, his eyes being rather weak.

Once Tommy stopped in his labor of cutting a big tree so that he might rest for a minute or two. On the very edge of the little clearing they had made, the moonlight fell on an old weather-gray log. Tommy stared at it a moment, then resumed his work. A few minutes later he chanced to look at it again. Somehow it seemed nearer than before. He stared long and hard, but it lay as motionless as a log should. Once more he resumed his work, but hardly had he done so when there was the warning thud of a neighbor's tail. Instantly Tommy scrambled for the water; and even as he did so, he caught a glimpse of that

They were prepared to rush for safety at the first warning. *Page 196.*

gray old log coming to life and leaping towards him. The instant he reached the water, he dived.

"What was it?" he whispered tremulously when, in the safety of the house, he touched noses with one of his neighbors.

"Tufty the Lynx," was the reply. "I smelled him and gave the warning. I guess it was lucky for you that I did."

"I guess it was," returned Tommy, with a shiver.

Another time, a huge black form sprang from the blacker shadows and caught one of the workers. It was a bear. Sometimes there would be three or four alarms in a night. So Tommy learned that the harvesting of the food supply was the most dangerous labor of all, for it took him farthest from the safety of the water.

At last this work was completed, and Tommy wondered if now they were to rest and idle away their time. But he did not have to wonder long. The old leader was not yet content, but must have the pond deepened all along the foot of the dam and around the entrances to the house. So now they once more turned to digging, this time under water, bringing the mud up to put on the dam or the house, some working on one and some on the other. The nights grew crisp and there was a hint of frost. It was then that they turned all their attention to the house, plastering it all over with mud save at the very top, where the air-holes were. So thick did they lay it on that only here and there did the end of a stick project. Then came a night which made a thin sheet of ice over the pond and froze the mud-plaster of the house. The cold increased. The ice grew thicker and the walls of the house so hard that not even the powerful claws of a bear could tear them open. It was for this that that last coating of mud had been put on.

The nights of labor were over at last. There was nothing to do now but sleep on the soft beds of grass or of thin splinters of wood, for some had preferred to make beds of this latter material. For exercise they swam in the quiet waters under the ice. When they were hungry, they slipped down through the water tunnel and out into the pond, swam to the food-pile, got a stick, and took it back to the house, where they gnawed the bark off in comfort and at their ease, afterward carrying the bare stick down to the dam for use in making repairs.

Once they discovered that the water was rapidly lowering. This meant a break in the dam. A trapper had cut a hole in it and cunningly placed a trap there. But the wise old leader knew all about traps, and the breach was repaired without harm to any one. Sometimes a lynx or a wolf would come across the ice and prowl around the house, sniffing hungrily as the smell of beaver came out through the tiny air-holes in the roof. But the thick walls were like rock, and Tommy and his companions never even knew of these hungry prowlers. Peace, safety, and contentment reigned under the ice of the beaver-pond.

But at last there came a day when a great noise reverberated under the ice. They knew not what it meant and lay shivering with fear. A long time they lay even after it had ceased. Then one of the boldest went for a stick from the food-pile. He did not return. Another went and he did not return. Finally Tommy went, for he was hungry. When he reached the food-pile, he found that it had been fenced in with stout poles driven down into the mud through holes cut in the ice. It was the cutting of these holes that had made the dreadful noise, though Tommy didn't know it. Around the food-pile he swam until at last he found an opening between the poles of the fence. He hesitated. Then, because he was very hungry, he entered. Hardly was he inside when another pole was thrust down through a hole behind him, and he was a prisoner under the ice inside that hateful fence.

Now a beaver must have air, and there was no air there and no way of getting any. Up above on the ice an Indian squatted. He knew just what was happening down below and he grinned. Beside him lay the two beavers who had preceded Tommy, drowned. Now Tommy was drowning. His lungs felt as if they would burst. Dully he realized that this was the end. As long as he could, he held his breath and then— Tommy came to himself with a frightened jump.

He was sitting on the old wishing-stone, and before him stretched the Green Meadows, joyous with happy life. He wasn't a beaver at all, but he knew that he had been a beaver, that he had lived the life of Paddy the Beaver. He could remember every detail of it, and he shuddered as he thought of those last dreadful minutes at the food-pile when he had felt himself drowning helplessly. Then the wonder of what he had learned grew upon him.

"Why," he exclaimed, "a beaver is an engineer, a lumberman, a dredger, a builder, and a mason! He's wonderful. He's the most wonderful animal in all the world!" His face clouded. "Why can't people leave him alone?" he exploded. "A man that will trap and kill one of those little chaps is worse than a lynx or a wolf. Yes, sir, that's what he is! Those critters kill to eat, but man kills just for the few dollars Paddy's fur coat will bring. When I grow up, I'm going to do something to stop trapping and killing. Yes, sir, that's what I'm going to do!"

Tommy got up and stretched. Then he started for home, and there was a thoughtful look on his freckled face. "Gee!" he exclaimed, "I've learned a pile this time. I didn't know there was so much pleasure in just work before. I guess I won't complain any more over what I have to do. I—I'm mighty glad I was a beaver for a little while, just for that." And then, whistling, Tommy headed straight for the wood-pile and his ax. He had work to do, and he was glad of it.

XII
Tommy Learns What It Is Like to Be a Bear

TOMMY'S thoughts were straying. Somehow they were straying most of the time these days. They had been, ever since that day when he had wished himself into a beaver. He dreamed of the Great Woods where rivers have their beginnings in gurgling brooks, and great lakes reflect moss-gray giants of the forest; where the beavers still ply their many trades unharmed by man, the deer follow paths of their own making, the otters make merry on their slipper-slides, the lynx pass through the dark shadows, themselves but grayer shadows, and bears go fishing, gather berries, and hunt the stored sweets of the bees. In short, the spell of the Great Woods, the wilderness unmarred by the hand of man, was upon Tommy.

Eagerly he read all that he could find about the feathered and furred folk who dwell there, and the longing to know more about them and their ways, to learn these things for himself, grew and grew. He wanted to hear things with his own ears and see things with his own eyes. Sometimes he went over to the Green Forest near his home and played that it was the Great Woods and that he was a mighty hunter. Then Happy Jack the Gray Squirrel became a fierce-eyed, tufted-eared, bob-tailed lynx, saucy Chatterer the Red Squirrel became a crafty fisher, the footprints of Reddy Fox grew in size to those of a wolf, Peter Rabbit was transformed into his cousin of the north, Jumper the Hare, and a certain old black stump was Buster Bear.

But it was only once in a while that Tommy played the hunter. Somehow, since he had learned so many things about the lives of the little feathered and furred people about him, he cared less and less about hunting them. So most often, when the Green Forest became the Great Woods, he was Buster Bear. That was more fun than being a hunter, much more fun. There was only one drawback—he didn't know as much about Buster Bear and his ways as he wished he did.

So now, as he trudged along towards the pasture to drive home the cows for the evening milking, his thoughts were straying to the Great Woods and Buster Bear. As he came to the old wishing-stone he glanced up at the sun. There was no need to hurry. He would have plenty of time to sit down there a while. So down he sat on the big gray rock and his thoughts went straying, straying deep into the Great Woods far from cows and milking and the woodpile just beyond the kitchen door. Bears never had to chop wood.

"I wish," said Tommy dreamily, "that I were a bear."

That was all, just a little spoken wish, but Tommy was no longer a dreamy boy with evening chores yet to be done. He was a little black furry animal, not unlike an overgrown puppy, following at the heels of a great gaunt black bear. In short, Tommy was a bear, himself. All about him was the beautiful wilderness, the Great Woods of his boyish dreams. Just behind him was another little bear, his twin sister, and the big bear was their mother.

Presently they came to an opening where there were no trees, but a tangle of brush. Years before, fire had swept through there, though Tommy knew nothing about that. In fact, Tommy knew little about anything as yet save that it was good, oh, so good, to be alive. On the edge of this opening Mother Bear paused and sat up on her haunches while she sniffed the air. The two little bears did the same thing. They didn't know why, but they did it because Mother Bear did. Then she dropped to all fours and told them to remain right where they were until she called them. They watched her disappear in the brush and waited impatiently. It seemed to them a very long time before they heard her call and saw her head above the bushes as she sat up, but really it was only a few minutes. Then they scampered to join her, each trying to be first.

When they reached her, such a glad sight as greeted them! All about were little bushes loaded with berries that seemed to have stolen their color from the sky. They were blueberries. With funny little squeals and grunts they stripped the berries

Just behind him was another little bear, his twin sister. *Page 204.*

from the bushes and ate and ate until they could eat no more. Then they wrestled with each other, and stood up on their hind legs and boxed until they were out of breath and glad to lie down for a rest while Mother Bear continued to stuff herself with berries.

It was very beautiful there in the Great Woods, and the two little bears just bubbled over with high spirits. They played hide-and-seek behind stumps and trees. They played tag. They chased each other up tall trees. One would climb to the top of a tall stump, and the other would follow and try to knock the first one off. Sometimes both would tumble down and land with a thump that would knock the breath from their little bodies. The bumps would hurt sometimes and make them squeal. This would bring Mother Bear in a hurry to see what had happened; and when she would find that no harm had come to them, she would growl a warning and sometimes spank them for giving her a fright.

But best of all they loved to wrestle and box, and, though they didn't know it, they were learning something. They were learning to be quick in their movements. They were learning how to strike swiftly and how to dodge quite as swiftly. Once in a while they would stand and not try to dodge, but see who could stand the hardest blow. And once in a while, I am sorry to say, they quarreled and fought. Then Mother Bear would take a hand and cuff and spank them until they squalled.

Very early they learned that Mother Bear was to be minded. Once she sent them up a tree and told them to stay there until she returned. Then she went off to investigate something which interested her. When she returned, the two little cubs were nowhere to be seen. They had grown tired of waiting for her to return and had come down to do a little investigating of their own. It didn't take her long to find them. Oh, my, no! And when she did—well, all the neighbors knew that two little cubs had disobeyed, and two little cubs were sure, very sure, that they never would do so again. Tommy was one.

At first, during those lovely summer days, Mother Bear never went far from them. You see, when they were very small, there were dangers. Oh, yes, there are dangers even for little bears. Tufty the Lynx would have liked nothing better than a meal of tender young bear, and Howler the Wolf would have rejoiced in an opportunity to snatch one of them without the risk of an encounter with Mother Bear. But Tommy and his sister grew fast, very fast. You see, there were so many good things to eat. Their mother dug for them the most delicious roots, tearing them from the ground with her great claws. It wasn't long before they had learned to find them for themselves and to dig them where the earth was soft enough. Then there were berries, raspberries and blackberries and blueberries, all they wanted, to be had for the gathering. And by way of variety there were occasional fish.

Tommy as a boy was very fond of fishing. As a bear he was quite as fond of it. On his first fishing-trip he got a wetting, a spanking, and no fish. It happened this way: Mother Bear had led them one moonlight night to a brook they never had visited before. Up the brook she led them until they reached a place where it was broad and shallow, the water gurgling and rippling over the stones and singing merrily. They were left in the brush on the edge of the brook where they could see and were warned to keep still and watch. Then Mother Bear stationed herself at a point where the water was just a wee bit deeper than elsewhere and ran a wee bit faster, for it had cut a little channel there. For a long time she sat motionless, a big black spot in the moonlight, which might have been a stump to eyes which had not seen her go there.

Tommy wondered what it all meant. For a long time, at least it was a long time to Tommy, nothing happened. The brook gurgled and sang and Mother Bear sat as still as the very rocks. Tommy began to get impatient. He was bubbling over with high spirits and sitting still was hard, very hard. Little by little he stole nearer to the water until he was on the very edge right behind Mother Bear. Then he caught a splash down the brook. He looked in that direction but could see nothing. Then there was another splash. He saw a silvery line and then made out a moving form. There was something alive coming up the brook. He edged over a little farther to see better.

Then Mother Bear stationed herself at a point where the water was just a wee bit deeper than elsewhere. *Page 208.*

There it was, coming nearer and nearer. Though he didn't know it then, it was a big trout working its way up the brook to the spring-holes higher up where the water was deep and cold.

In the shallowest places the fish was sometimes half out of water. It was making straight for the little channel where Mother Bear sat. Nearer it came. Suddenly Mother Bear moved. Like lightning one of her big paws struck down and under, scooping the trout out and sending it flying towards the shore. Alas for Tommy! He was directly in the way. The fish hit him full in the face, fell back in the water, wriggled and jumped frantically—and was gone. Tommy was so startled that he gave a frightened little whimper. And then a big black paw descended and sent him rolling over and over in the water. Squalling lustily, wet, frightened and miserable, Tommy scrambled to his feet and bolted for the shore where he hid in in the brush.

"I didn't mean to!" he kept whimpering as he watched Mother Bear return to her fishing. Presently another trout came along and was sent flying up on the shore. Then Tommy watched his obedient sister enjoy a feast while he got not so much as a taste. After that they often went fishing on moonlight nights. Tommy had learned his lesson and knew that fish were the reward of patience, and it was not long before he was permitted to fish for himself.

Sometimes they went frogging along the marshy shores of a little pond. This was even more fun than

Sometimes they went frogging along the
marshy shores of a little pond. *Page 210.*

fishing. It was great sport to locate a big frog by the sound of his deep bass voice and then softly steal up and cut a "chugarum" short, right in the middle. Then when he had eaten his fill, it was just as much fun to keep on hunting them just to see them plunge with long frightened leaps into the water. It tickled Tommy immensely, and he would hunt them by the hour just for this.

One day Mother Bear led them to an old dead tree half rotted away at the bottom. While they sat and looked on in round-eyed wonder, she tore at the rotten wood with her great claws. Almost at once the air about her was full of insects humming angrily. Tommy drew nearer. A sharp pain on the end of his nose made him jump and squeal. Another shooting pain in one ear brought another squeal and he slapped at the side of his head. One of those humming insects dropped at his feet. It must be that it had had something to do with that pain. Tommy beat a retreat into the brush. But Mother Bear kept on clawing at the tree, growling and whining and stopping now and then to slap at the insects about her. By and by the tree fell with a crash. It partly split when it struck the ground. Then Mother Bear put her great claws into the crack and tore the tree open, for you know she was very strong. Tommy caught a whiff of something that made his mouth water. Never in all his short life had he smelled anything so delicious. He forgot all about the pain in his nose and his ear and came out of his hiding-place.

Another shooting pain in one ear brought
another squeal. *Page 212.*

Mother Bear thrust a great paw into the tree and tore out a piece of something yellow and dripping and tossed it in Tommy's direction.

There were a lot of those insects crawling over it, but Tommy didn't mind. The smell of it told him that it must be the best thing that ever was, better than berries, or fish, or frogs, or roots. And with the first taste he knew that his nose had told the truth. It was honey! It didn't take Tommy a minute to gobble up honey, comb, bees and all. Then, heedless of stings, he joined Mother Bear. What were a few stings compared to such delicious sweets? So he learned that dead trees are sometimes of interest to bears. They ate and ate until Tommy's little stomach was swelled out like a little balloon. Then they rolled on the ground to crush the bees clinging to their fur, after which Mother Bear led them to a muddy place on the shore of a little pond, and the cool mud took out the fire of the stings. Later, Tommy learned that not all bee-trees could be pulled down in this way, but that sometimes they must be climbed and ripped open with the claws of one paw while he held on with the other and endured the stings of the bees as best he could. But the honey was always worth all it cost to get.

Next to feasting on honey Tommy enjoyed most a meal of ants, particularly red ants; and this seems queer, because red ants are as sour as honey is sweet. But it was so. Any kind of ants would do, but red ants were best. And ants were easier to find and to get than honey. The latter he had only once in a while, but ants he had every day. He found them, thousands of them, under and in rotting old logs and in decayed old stumps. He seldom passed an old log without trying to roll it over. If he succeeded, he was almost sure to find a frightened colony of ants rushing about frantically. A few sweeps of his long tongue, a smacking of his lips and he moved on. Sometimes he found grubs or fat beetles, and these, though not so good as the ants, were always acceptable on his bill of fare. And he dearly loved to hunt wood-mice. It was almost as much fun as fishing or frogging.

So the long summer passed happily, and Tommy grew so fast that presently he became aware that not even Tufty the Lynx willingly crossed his path. He could go and come unafraid of any of the wilderness dwellers and forgot what fear was until a never-forgotten day in the early fall. He had followed Mother Bear to a certain place where late blueberries still clung to the bushes. As she reached the edge of the opening, she stopped short and lifted her nose, wrinkling the skin of it as she tested the air. Tommy did the same. He had great faith in what his nose could tell him. The wind brought to him now a strange smell unlike any he had known, an unpleasant smell. Somehow, he didn't know why, it gave him a queer prickly feeling all over. He looked at Mother Bear. She was staring out into the blueberry patch, and her lips were drawn back in an ugly way, showing her great teeth. Tommy looked out in the berry-patch. There were two strange two-legged creatures, gathering berries. They were not nearly as big as Mother Bear and they didn't look dangerous. He stared at them curiously. Then he turned to look at Mother Bear. She was stealing away so silently that not even a leaf rustled. She was afraid!

Tommy followed her, taking care not to make the least sound. When they were at a safe distance, he asked what it meant. "Those were men," growled Mother Bear deep down in her throat, "and that was the man-smell. Whenever you smell that, steal away. Men are the only creatures you have to fear; but whatever you do, keep away from them. They are dangerous."

After that, Tommy continually tested the air for the dreaded man-smell. Several times he caught it. Once from a safe hiding-place he watched a fisherman and another time a party of campers, but he took care that they should not suspect that he was near. By late fall he was so big that he began to feel independent and to wander off by himself. Almost every day he would stand up to a tree, reach as far up as he could, and dig his claws into the bark to see how tall he was. But when he found the measuring tree of a bigger bear, he took care not to put his mark there and usually stole away where he would not be likely to meet the maker of the high mark.

With the falling of the beechnuts Tommy found a new and delicious food and stuffed himself. These days he roamed far and wide and explored all the country for miles around. He grew fat and, as the weather grew colder, his coat grew thicker. He learned much about his neighbors and their ways, and his sense of humor led him often to give them scares just for the fun of seeing them jump and run.

With the coming of the first snow a strange desire to sleep stole over him. He found a great tree which had been torn up by the roots in some wind storm and about which smaller trees had fallen, making a great tangle. Under the upturned roots of the great tree was a hollow, and into this he scraped leaves and the branches of young balsams which he broke off. Thus he made a comfortable bed and with a sigh of contentment lay down to sleep. The snow fell and drifted over his bedroom, but he knew nothing of that. The cold winds, the bitter winds, swept through the wilderness, and the trees cracked with the cold, but Tommy slept on. Days slipped into weeks and weeks into months and still he slept. He would not waken until gentle spring melted the snow unless—

"Moo-oo!"

Tommy's eyes flew wide open. For a full minute he stared blinkingly out over the Green Meadows. Then with a jump he came to his feet. "My gracious, it's getting late, and those cows are wondering what has become of me!" he exclaimed. He hurried towards the pasture, breaking into a run, for it was milking-time. But his thoughts were far away. They were in the Great Woods. "I've been a bear!" he exclaimed triumphantly, "and I know just how he lives and feels, and why he loves the Great Woods so. Of all the critters I've been since I found out about the old wishing-stone, I'd rather be Buster Bear than any one, next to being just what I am. He has more fun than any one I know of and nothing and nobody to fear but man."

Tommy's brow clouded for an instant. "It's a shame," he blurted out, "that every living thing is afraid of man! And—and I guess it's his own fault. They needn't ever be afraid of me, I can tell them that! That old wishing-stone has taught me a lot, and I ain't never going to forget how it feels to be hunted and afraid all the time."

And Tommy never has.

THE END.